Garlands

of

Peace

Garlands

of

Peace

Two Novelettes and a Novella by

Malania E. Reynolds

THREE SKILLET

GARLANDS OF PEACE, Reynolds, Malania E.

First Edition

 THREE SKILLET

www.ThreeSkilletPublishing.com

Cover design by Farley L Dunn

ISBN: 978-1-943189-68-7

Contents

Abbot's Farm

The Good Fight

The Law and Miss Eliza

Abbot's Farm

— 1 —

Marantha Talley watched with fascination as the water droplets from the storm overhead hit the window pane. The dreary day matched her mood. Then, every day felt gray and lifeless, with her Jeffrey gone. Through the glass, gray clouds billowed against a darkening sky, sending threats of stronger storms to come.

With excruciating slowness, she watched raindrop after raindrop slide down to join the building puddles of water accumulating at the bottom of the sill.

Only half her mind was on the cup of tepid tea in her hand. The design on the fragile china service was of blue flowers, heavily applied, and with green leaves along the base. She rubbed a leaf with her thumb and imagined it was a real flower captured in the glaze. She could hear the drone of voices in the background but didn't care what the women were saying. They wouldn't ordinarily have tea in the afternoon, but the preacher had come to call, and her mother was always one for the proprieties.

It wasn't especially good tea. With the war, makings for the drink were scarce. Sugar was even more so, making this a foul beverage, indeed.

She sipped the bitter brew and watched as a small brown bird landed on a bare branch of the tree outside. It fluttered its wings and flew away. That was her, she thought. Solitary, alone and cold.

She wished she could forget her sorrow and fly away.

It had been a month since she had received the letter from the Adjutant General's office informing her that her husband, Jeffrey James Talley, had been killed in battle in a place called Shiloh in faraway Tennessee.

For a whole month her family had tried to give her solace, but she couldn't forget the horrible day when he had marched off to war. He'd stood, proud in his new blue uniform, with a smile on his face. The family had gathered around, wishing him well.

She hated the memory of it, just as she'd hated returning to her mother's house because of it.

He'd joined up as soon as the regiment was formed, bragging that he would be back in a few weeks. But, he didn't make it. He was buried in the soil of a foreign land, and the sting of tears that haunted her were all she could cling to as she lay in her bed at night, soaking her pillow until she slept in exhaustion.

She leaned forward and carefully placed the cup and saucer on the table in front of her. She felt life stir inside her. She gently placed her hand on her belly. Her chenille dress of black silk was far too fancy for a mother-to-be, yet with her husband only a month dead, she'd had little choice in what was available to wear. Her poor child would never know its father. What did her dress matter? The child would never hear the deep bass sound of his voice as he sang in the church choir.

Marantha, who went by Maddie, drew in a deep breath and steeled herself. She really must pull herself together. Proper etiquette dictated that she should listen to the preacher and her mother and at least try to follow along.

She plastered a smile on her face and forced herself to concentrate.

The reverend Mr. Charles Kitsfield was a tall, thin man with a protruding Adam's apple. A clean-shaven chin contrasted with his bushy side whiskers. His black frock coat and white shirt fit him poorly; and his pale, bony wrists protruded as he took a sip of his tea. His hand seemed enormous as he held the delicate tea cup. It was an open secret that he wore clothes from the charity barrel sent each year from the headquarters of the Baptist Mission Society in Connecticut. Insufficient funds to maintain a family in the towns to which he was sent to minister made the reverend as poor as those to whom he ministered. He didn't complain, however, for at least he had kind neighbors like Walindra Foster to offer him tea and cake on a Sunday afternoon.

"Mrs. Foster, I'm so happy I've found a solution to your little problem." Kitsfield smiled broadly, pleased with himself.

Maddie's attention perked up, and she took in her mother's full appearance. She was a short, plump woman in her early fifties. Her dress touted a wide, white collar, over a pale green chiffon. Large bows tied her sleeves at her elbows, and her skirts fanned out around her. The tips of her shoes revealed elegantly sewn organza over leather soles with brass buckles to give them shine. She had been a Walker in her youth and accustomed to a fine, luxurious home and servants. She forced herself into the affairs of her neighbors and society with her commanding will and tendency to gossip.

What problem could her mother possibly have? Maddie listened more carefully.

"I have found a husband for Mrs. Talley!" Kitsfield nodded at the young, freshly widowed woman and back to her mother. "When you first approached me about the matter, I was quite hopeful, for there are several single men in the parish who would appreciate the honor of having a charming, lovely young widow like your daughter as their wife."

"A husband? What do you mean, Preacher? I don't need a husband." Maddie was horrified, and she felt her self-control begin to evaporate.

"But," Kitsfield blustered, now confused. "Your mother just spoke with me—"

Maddie was having none of it. "Mama, what have you done? Jeffrey's only been gone a month." She felt dizzy and brought her hand to her forehead to still the pounding in her temple.

Elizabeth Foster, her younger sister, came to sit beside her on the pale blue brocade sofa with its horsehair stuffing and intricately carved backpieces, took her hand in hers and patted her on the back in sympathy, but Maddie didn't want to be touched. She needed an answer.

She drew herself up and sat erect on the seat, determined to be strong and forceful.

"Now, Maddie, I won't have this hysteria." Mrs. Foster spoke with a no-nonsense tone in her voice, as she toyed with an ivory and teak fan on the tall side table adjoining her chair. She opened it without looking at her hands and began to fan her neck. "You've been carrying on like you're the only one who's suffered in this war. I can't continue to support you on my widow's pension. Do you think that I haven't suffered from the loss of a husband's support? You must think of your brothers' and sisters' welfare."

"Mama—" Maddie began, only to be interrupted.

"You listen to me, Daughter. Jane and Elizabeth must be given their rightful share of your father's estate for a dowry, and Johnnie and Samuel must have a proper education. Janie must have new clothes. It was alright to take you in when that foolish boy went off to war, but you can't stay longer. We must think of the future!" She snapped the fan closed and set it aside.

Maddie didn't realize tears were sliding down her cheeks until she felt a drop on her hand. She'd felt guilty moving in with her mother and siblings when Jeffrey went away, but they thought it would only be for a few weeks. She reached to dry her tears and felt the baby kick again.

She moaned in pain and despair.

Kitsfield turned to Mrs. Foster in embarrassment. He leaned in and whispered, "What am I to do? I've given my word to the prospective groom, and I can't go to him with a refusal of my offer of marriage."

Mrs. Foster patted his hand. "I'm sure it will work

out."

"I suppose," he replied. Then, with an unctuous smile, he plunged back into the conversation. "Mrs. Foster, Mrs. Talley, I've given my word to Douglas Abbot that the wedding will take place. What shall I say to him?"

The preacher's ears were red and his Adam's apple seemed to have a life of its own, bouncing up and down in his slender neck. It was too much, and Maddie jumped from her seat and almost toppled the table in front of her.

"Douglas Abbot? That's the man you've chosen for me? But, he must be fifty years old and has gray hair. How could you think I would marry such an old man? And, he has children of his own. Oh, Mama, I can't marry Douglas Abbot!" Maddie wailed her insistence in her anger and pain. She clasped her hands so tightly together that she felt the bite of her nails into her palm, and she took a deep breath to calm herself.

"Mrs. Talley, he's offered to care for your child as his own and to pay the bride's fee to your mother. He needs a mother for his three daughters. You'll have a good home for your unborn child." Kitsfield turned from one woman to another, trying to decipher which he should address in his attempt to persuade the young widow to accept his choice of husband for her.

"Money? That's what this is about? My mother says that she can't support me, and Douglas Abbot has offered to pay her for my services as wife and mother of his children? What about me and my feelings, my lost love for my husband? How can you be so callous and uncaring, Mama?"

"Sit down, Maddie, and calm yourself. It's you who's

being selfish and unkind to your family. You always were high strung and emotional. Now, I'll have no more of this nonsense. You'll marry Douglas Abbot, or you'll find yourself out in the streets begging for food."

Maddie sat down, overcome with despair. She couldn't believe this was happening, her own mother calling her selfish and emotional.

She covered her face with her hands and cried.

"What's all this yelling about? What's wrong, Maddie?"

Samuel, the eldest son and the smartest of Maddie's siblings, appeared in the room. He wore navy trousers over laced, black shoes, with a short jacket in bright blue. The sleeves were bound with cording to match his trousers. His shirt was a pale-yellow seersucker, with a tall collar tied with a thin scarf.

Maddie took her hands from her face and looked at her handsome, tall brother. He, too, had suffered because of the war; enlisting on the same day as her husband, he had contracted dysentery and was released from service after a few months. He was still pale and weakened from the disease. When he discovered the preacher sitting in his father's stuffed cowhide chair, and his sister on the sofa with her head in her hands, he paused in front of his sister.

"I was in my bedroom, and I heard the sounds of an argument. I've come to investigate. Maddie, what's wrong?"

"Do you think I'm selfish, Sammie? Have I been a burden to you and the family these last few months? Tell me honestly." She looked at him beseechingly from water-soaked eyes.

Samuel looked at his mother and at the preacher. "Why would they think you selfish, Sister? I don't understand. Mama, what's going on in here?"

"Samuel, sit down. Why does everyone want to tower over me like this? Have a seat, and I'll explain." Many women in Mrs. Foster's matron's club would have trembled at the sound of her voice, had she addressed them in that manner. Her son wasn't so timid, but even so, Samuel sat and folded his hands in his lap.

There was a commotion at the door, and Janie and Johnnie, the twins, burst in unannounced.

"What's going on, here, Mama? We heard you arguing from the kitchen. Even Russell and Ivy heard you. Do you think it's proper for the servants to listen to such caterwauling in this house?" Johnnie Foster was prim and of average height, a young man who believed in talking bluntly. He was in a gentleman's suit, with a hint of a tail, and grey striped trousers under a darker gray jacket. His shoes were black overlaid with white, and he wore a thick, folded kerchief in his breast pocket. He felt it his duty to protect and care for his mother. He was studying to be an attorney like his father and had begun to take on the characteristics of his mentor, Judge Bartholomew, who was a pompous, arrogant man with white hair and a full beard. Johnnie took in the scene in a glance, Mama sitting stiffly and dominant near the fireplace, Maddie and Elizabeth on the sofa, both with streaks of tears on their cheeks, Sammie sitting with his hands folded in polite attention, and the preacher.

Janie wore a high-waisted gown of pink organza, with a woven shawl to cover her shoulders. Without the shawl, the cut was inappropriate for daytime wear, but her mother allowed it, as long as she was covered.

Her shoes were pale pink silk, designed for indoor wear.

Of everyone in the room, it was the preacher who was most out of place.

"Please, everyone, sit down. Janie, you'll have to take the footstool. Oh, my, there doesn't seem to be enough chairs. Sammie, ring for Russell to bring another." Mrs. Foster took her white handkerchief from her pocket and pretended to sniff into it.

"No, Mama," Sammie declared with determination. "I won't disturb the servants. You were about to tell me why you think Maddie's selfish and why she's been crying." He stood and offered his spot for Janie, and she sat, leaving Johnnie to find his way to the footstool. Sammie stood in front of the fireplace and gave the preacher an inquiring glare.

Janie giggled, amused for some reason, and Johnnie turned to Maddie with a look of bewilderment and surprise.

"Mama?" He stood and looked at his mother. "This is too much. Maddie, selfish? Why, she's the most generous person in the world. Why's Mr. Kitsfield here today? We need to understand just what's going on."

The room had turned into bedlam. Kitsfield coughed and looked at the carpet, shifting his eyes away from a small rent in the surface.

"Johnnie, Sammie, please, it's all a mistake, I'm sure. The preacher has kindly found a husband for Maddie, but she refuses to accept the offer of marriage. She says

Douglas Abbot's too old and has children."

"Oh, Mama, it's true." Maddie began to sob once more.

"Now, Daughter," Mrs. Foster scolded her. She turned back to her son. "She's with child, and I can't keep her longer. I've said that she must marry and leave this house for the good of the rest of the family." She put the handkerchief to her nose and sniffled. She gazed around her to see how her children would react. "You understand that she has my sympathy over the loss of her husband, but we can't maintain her and the coming child forever. She must assume some responsibility for her situation."

Johnnie looked at Maddie with speculation in his gray eyes. He looked at his twin, but Janie was staring at her sister in consternation. Elizabeth wore a face of compassion and grief. Sammie was shocked and looked at his mother in fascination.

"Douglas Abbot?" Sammie was outraged and glared at the preacher with loathing. "You've proposed that Maddie marry Douglas Abbot? He's nothing but a farmer and works with hogs and goats. You don't know what you're doing, Reverend Kitsfield, to think that my sister would accept the offer of a common farmer for a husband."

"Ah, but brother. He's a very wealthy farmer and has a great deal of influence with the town council and local merchants. Remember last year when the council wanted to raise money for a new fire truck? It was Farmer Abbot who persuaded the townspeople to hold a carnival and raise the funds. And, you see the results. The new fire truck sits in the field next to the municipal court building. I can't see what the age of the man has to do with marriage. She

20

would have a good home in which to raise her child." Johnnie looked at his mother, and he could see the approval in her eyes.

"There, you see? Johnnie agrees with me. Maddie must leave and find her own life outside of this house." Mrs. Foster glanced at the preacher with justification in her eyes.

"But, Mama. A farmer! What will your society friends think of your eldest daughter living in an old weathered farm house in the country with hogs and chicken and cows? Won't they whisper and gossip about her behind our backs?" Sammie was adamant that society wouldn't accept his sister in their circle because of her projected lowered status among them. The fact that Douglas Abbot had great wealth wouldn't persuade the old women to accept her as an equal to them.

"Oh, but it's true, Mama! You can't suppose that Maddie will be happy with a man twice her age. Johnnie, you must remember that she lost her husband and best friend in the war. Poor Jeffrey lies in a cold grave in Tennessee, and you've forgotten the way he looked in his fine uniform when he went to fight for us in the war. You can't expect her to marry so soon, when you can see that she's grieving for him." Elizabeth was a timid creature and rarely spoke up in family quarrels, but she felt that her sister was being rushed into something that she wasn't ready to accept.

Kitsfield interrupted in confusion, speaking as much to the children as to their mother. "When your mother came to me for advice and the name of a man willing to marry her daughter, I thought the whole family was in agreement with the change in her status, but I can see that it's not so.

21

I hadn't thought of Mrs. Talley's husband only gone for a month. Surely, the woman should have some time to grieve for her loss. On the other hand, as a family man myself, I can see that Douglas Abbot desperately needs a wife and mother for his daughters. He's agreed to the arrangement, and I don't see how Marantha wouldn't benefit from the support of a man in her present circumstances."

Maddie listened to everyone and came to realize that she was causing them to take sides against each other in the debate. She couldn't let her family continue to argue in this manner. She tried to picture Douglas Abbot in her mind and couldn't recall his face; only his tall stature and strong shoulders and arms. He was a member of the same congregation, and she'd seen him with his three daughters in tow. He often had his aunt Cornelia at his side, moving about with the other men and ladies of the congregation.

She didn't remember ever having spoken to him personally.

She felt the lump at her waist with her hand and thought of the future of her child. She knew hardly anything about the man, but she did know that he was a kindly, indulgent father to his children. A rolling movement started in her side and moved to her navel, and she almost screamed with the pressure it exerted against her hand. The child would be born soon, and she must think of him, not herself. She looked at her mother, who was speaking, but Maddie didn't hear the words, only saw the look of anger on her face. Clearly, she must relieve her mother of the burden she had caused by her presence in the house. She glanced at the thin, embarrassed face of the preacher and took a deep breath.

"Stop! Please, Mama, don't say more!" Everyone turned to look at her, and her face grew warm. She felt dizzy and nauseous but held her head high and proud. "Preacher Kitsfield, please tell Douglas Abbot that I will marry him as soon as it can be arranged. Mama, I'm sorry if I've caused you pain or discomfort while in your home. I won't continue to be a burden to you and the family. Please forgive me."

She walked from the room with the grace of a duchess. The family began to speak at once, but she didn't hear them. She went upstairs to the small room that had been given to her when her husband had gone to war and left her in her parent's home. She began to pack a few clothes in the old faded and tattered carpetbag in which they had traveled those lovely months ago when her husband was so alive and valiant.

Someone knocked at the door, but she didn't answer, and after a few minutes they went away. She was left alone in the room for the rest of the day. She didn't go down to the dining room knowing they would be talking about her. Ivy, the somber-faced domestic servant, brought her a meal on a tray, and she ate it at the table by the window while watching the rain fall silently on the grass, the trees, and the roof of the house next door.

She wondered if it also fell on the newly dug grave of her lover in faraway Tennessee.

— 2 —

Douglas Abbot slogged through the mud of his barn-yard, making his way toward the pig pen. The wooden fencing glistened with accumulated moisture, but the portion under the tin roofing he'd installed was dry and dusty. It had been a substantial investment in the new material, but it kept the hay in his barn secure and dry. The walls of the structure were board and batten, whitewashed, but not too recently. With the continued rain, it might be another summer before it got another application. Still, the wood was sound, with no rot, and it was as sturdy a barn as anywhere in the county.

His boots made sucking sounds as they fell and rose in the slime and water caused by the rain. The cold water seeped inside the collar of his woolen jacket. He pulled the old felt hat around his ears to lessen the flow, but it didn't help.

He held a bucket of slop in one hand, sour milk and leftovers from the breakfast his aunt had prepared for his children and himself. The smell was rank but just what the pigs loved.

When he had announced at Sunday dinner, over his aunt Cornelia's carefully prepared boiled ham, sliced and fried potatoes, and freshly baked bread, that he was being remarried, she had swollen like a toad and accused him of ungratefulness and selfishness.

"How?" he'd asked incredulously. He'd expected her to be glad for him, and perhaps grateful to have extra help around the house.

"I came to care for your daughters when your wife, Charity, died two years ago. All this time I've worked for you for nothing but room and board. However, I won't live in a house where I'm not wanted or needed."

He regretted that Cornelia thought she must leave the family. She'd begun gathering the dishes from the table as she talked, carelessly clattering them together, a sure sign of her anger. The argument had lasted for over an hour, with Douglas trying to explain his loneliness and grief, and his need for a wife, as Cornelia roughly scrubbed the kitchen utensils, counters, tabletops, and any other surfaces she could find to keep from looking at him.

Cornelia adamantly said that she wouldn't be considered a servant under a new mistress in the household. She had thrown down her wash cloth, slapped his face and drawn back in shock, her hand quivering at her bad behavior. She had cried, and he had consoled her, but she wouldn't change her mind.

She'd packed her bags, one a cloth carpetbag, and the

25

second a wooden trunk of no mean size bound with leather straps. She was leaving on the morning train.

Her abrupt decision had Douglas feeding the hogs and milking the cow early this morning, so he could take her to the train station. The wedding was planned for noon, and he had many things to do before that time, but he wouldn't let his beloved aunt go without a proper good-bye.

She was now in the house dressing for the trip, having already gotten the girls ready. She was returning to Kingsborough, to live with her younger sister and her husband. He prayed that she would be happy in her new situation, although he'd rather she changed her mind and stayed with him.

Douglas left the contents of the bucket in the trough for the hogs, scattered corn on the ground for the chickens and milked the cow. He walked back to the house absorbed in despair mixed with hope and excitement. What would it be like to again have a wife in the house; a mother for his daughters? He didn't know Maddie well; only from a distance when they met as fellow members of the church at worship service. He had known her husband, Jeffrey, as a strong proponent of the Northern cause for which he'd fought and died.

Douglas had been too old to join up, but he wouldn't have gone anyway, leaving his daughters alone with only his aunt to care for them. He and Charity had discussed it before she passed. What should he do if a war started? She was strongly opposed to slavery, even though she'd been born and bred in the South. She'd begged him not to leave her, and he hadn't. That spring she'd sickened from the birth of their fourth child, and she and the baby boy had died when it was born.

The preacher had suggested to Douglas that Maddie needed a husband to support her in her grief over her fallen soldier, as well as a father for her unborn child. It seemed an opportunity he couldn't pass by. He hoped the unborn child was a male. He wanted a boy so badly to carry his name and to help him around the farm. His heart pounded with excitement as he entered the back door of the house. The wooden floorboards were rough but clean, thanks to Cornelia. Several places were stained, one where an ember had jumped from the stove, and another where Charity, his first wife, had dropped a whole, cooked ham from the oven, because of the heat. The event had frightened Sally, no more than seven or eight at the time, and she'd burst into tears. Charity had wiped the meat down, and they'd enjoyed it for supper anyway, slowly easing Sally's tears. The grease, however, had formed a stain that had become permanent.

Now, one of the girls was crying upstairs. Without rushing, but quickly and efficiently, he strained and poured the fresh milk into a glass pitcher and carried it down the steps to the cool root cellar, covering it with cheesecloth to keep it fresh. The earthy smell of the vegetables comforted him, seeing them as the just reward of the labor of his hands. Corn, still in the husks, a bowl of tomatoes, which would be sliced and fried, and several of last year's apples, though they had begun to shrivel. The crying continued, and he could tell it was Sally, his eldest and most sensitive daughter, who was in tears. There was nothing to be done for it, so he finished his early morning chores and went

27

upstairs to change clothes. By the time he ascended the stairs, the crying had stopped.

The trip to the train station was unpleasant. He felt betrayed that Cornelia wouldn't change her mind and attend his wedding ceremony. She sat stiff and defiant until the last moment, when she broke down in tears and hugged and kissed everyone. Sally cried the whole time, her tears almost breaking her father's heart, but to no avail, for he'd made a commitment and wouldn't change his mind. Nellie, the next to the youngest at eight years, was bewildered. She couldn't understand why her aunt Cornelia had to leave. She was named for her aunt and felt a special bond because of it.

The youngest daughter, Abby, age three, was half asleep. She'd been awakened before dawn and told to get dressed. Auntie had forced her to rise and stand while she dressed the child in her finest frock of white-eye lace and brown shoes. She dozed on the way to the station and cried when Cornelia, with her hair pulled severely from her face and tied with a gold ribbon, and her navy seersucker shirt tucked firmly into a cream skirt that topped tall, no-nonsense, button-up boots, boarded the train.

It was a troubling time for Douglas, but he returned to the farmyard with two hours to spare before the wedding.

He had no time to himself, however, for the guests began to arrive while he was brushing Sally's hair. Mrs. Parthenia Pembrook, her husband Arthur, and her sister Gertrude Justine, a spinster, arrived and took charge of the girls and the food. Parthenia was in an orange-trimmed frock of pressed linen, with a great hat filled with flowers. Gertrude was dressed more sedately, with a rose-colored skirt and a white, short jacket, and a lime, ruffled blouse. Her hat was a simple bowl wrapped with a ribbon. Arthur wore a Sunday suit in dark cord, with a vest of embroidered farm animals, showing anyone with pride, if they wished to ask. They'd just spread the cloth on the table in the large dining room when Frankie Wilcox came in the door with her famous pot roast and brown gravy, and a spice cake. She was dressed in a trim, white skirt under a kelly green overshirt, with large, silk buttons in a lighter shade. Her hat sported a stuffed bird on a branch intertwined with real leaves. Frankie was a widow who had fostered a hope of winning Douglas Abbot for herself. But, she was happy for him, or so she said to those who would listen. She intended to shift her attention onto Wallace Griffith, who was better looking, but not as wealthy.

Sally, with her eyes red and swollen from her tears, looked with suspicion at the members of the bridal party. She didn't understand at age ten why her father wanted to marry, if it caused her beloved aunt Cornelia to leave. She seemed determined to be as contrary as possible to punish the new lady for breaking up her peaceful family life.

No one reminded her how she had often heard her parents arguing through the night, and the signs of unhappiness on her mother's face the next morning. Somehow, death had brought only glad memories of the loved one who had passed on.

Mrs. Marantha Talley—Maddie—arrived in a two-person Goddard buggy with a half top beside her brother Samuel. The rest of her family emerged from a four-person carriage with a full leather top, followed by a flatback wagon pulled by a mule with Maddie's worldly goods stacked on the back. Even for her marriage, she refused to wear bright colors, although her mother and sisters had teased and tormented her to discard her black widow's garments for the occasion. She wouldn't cast aside her feelings and grief for the neighbors and congregants of the church to whisper and gossip about. If they chose to forget Jeffrey Talley and his sacrifice for his country, she wouldn't. It caused a stir among the guests, but Douglas refused to speak of it. He was nervous and excited, as well as frustrated with Sally's attitude.

Nellie and Abby clung to him with sticky fingers and dirty faces. Gertrude Justine, a local school teacher, took them away and cleaned them up. She told them amusing stories that made them laugh. Soon a few of the other children joined them in the laughter.

The contrast between the bride and the women of her family was startling. Mrs. Foster moved among the guests with her usual aplomb and ignored the comments and mockery of her neighbors. Elizabeth wore pink; Janie wore a pale green frock and an enormous hat, more suitable for a spring garden party.

Johnnie Foster was somber and stiff in manner and dress. Samuel was friendly and good-hearted. He opposed this marriage but was determined to support his sister in her decision. The men carried the bride's trunk, carpetbag and hat boxes into the house and placed them in what looked like the groom's bedroom.

Douglas, as the groom, spoke his pledge to his wife with a deep male rumble; Maddie, as the bride, was hesitant but resolute. Kitsfield gave a long-winded sermon on duty and responsibility which made some of the male guests uncomfortable, but they shrugged it aside when the food and punch began to appear. The dancing was lively, with a fiddle, banjo and guitar beating out the rhythm for the participants with enthusiasm, if not with talent.

The more strait-laced ladies of the Matron's Benevolent Society frowned their disapproval at the gaiety, when told the bride's former husband hadn't been dead above a month. The men found a secret bottle in one of the merchants' wagons and shunned the punch. The children ran and played in the mud with abandon. At least the rain had stopped, one man commented, and the sun had begun to shine.

Frankie Wilcox twittered and threw herself at Wallace Griffith, until that gentleman, flushed with embarrassment, mounted his horse and rode away. Frankie simply shrugged and started after Claude Dawkins, a blond-haired, blue-eyed bachelor five years her junior. He didn't seem to object to the attention, and they were last seen walking toward the barn. The other ladies laughed, gossiped and waved their fans before their lips, vastly entertained by Frankie's antics.

When the shadows grew long in the yard, the men remembered there were chores to be done, and a few at a time, in carriages, wagons and on horseback, the guests began to leave. The music stopped, and the neighbor children grew cranky and tired, whining for their mothers. They were gathered in the arms of their parents and whisked to their individual methods of transportation.

Mrs. Foster came to say goodbye and attempted to hug her daughter, but Maddie simply said, "Goodbye, Mama," and turned to thank Sammie and Johnnie for helping with the luggage. She gave Elizabeth and Janie a peck on the cheek and turned to Douglas, who had quietly slipped up beside her. She took his arm and plastered a smile on her face, as she bid farewell to the other guests. She ignored the look of puzzlement and anger in her mother's eyes.

The last to leave was a reluctant Gertrude Justine and her sister, Mrs. Pembrook, and her husband. The first to arrive and the last to go, they had made sure that the kitchen was clean and food left in the oven for the family's supper. Gertrude had helped the girls change out of their good clothes into something more suitable for play. She left them with a picture book, paper and pencil to entertain them. She told Sally and Nellie she would see them in the school room soon. Douglas and Maddie thanked them politely and stood as they rode away in the carriage.

Silence descended as the husband and wife were alone for the first time.

"I wonder what happened to Frankie Wilcox and Claude Dawkins? Do you suppose they're still in the barn?" Maddie smiled in a mischievous way at the thought of the couple in the hay loft. She turned and gave Douglas a wink.

Douglas was amazed at the wink. He'd thought his new wife sober and genteel. He grabbed her around the waist and pulled her into his arms. He kissed her hard on the lips, and she didn't draw back. He swung her around, and she laughed. He turned to the door and was just opening it, when a disheveled Frankie and a coatless, tieless Claude appeared at the barn door. The two couples looked at each other keenly. Claude waved cheerfully, tied his horse to Frankie's wagon and drove away. Douglas waved as they passed from their sight.

The kitchen was tidy, and the scent of leftover food and coffee permeated the room. Douglas picked up Maddie in his arms and carried her to the stairs. He put her down in his bedroom and kissed her passionately. The sound of a horrified gasp alerted him to the presence of his daughter, Sally, in the doorway. She screamed and ran from the room. He shrugged and followed her, an apology in his eyes.

Undaunted, Maddie removed her hat and leaned to untie the high-topped shoes that pinched her toes. She could barely reach them since her belly protruded so far. It was tight around her waist, and uncomfortable, but she managed to remove her shoes and stockings. She found her carpetbag where Sammie and Johnnie had left it and withdrew a large pink-and-green gingham dress with no waist binding. She pulled the black mourning dress over her head and sighed. She took off her undergarments, leaving only a thin chemise. It was such a relief to be free of the restrictions of society. She donned the colorful dress and a pair of flannel slippers and walked downstairs to explore her new home. As she went, she heard a man's voice and the voices of his daughters. She looked at the new, shiny ring on her finger and sighed again.

She took her time wandering from room to room of the large, rambling farm house. The floors squeaked as she walked, and she noticed there was a carpet only in the parlor, one that didn't reach to the walls. It was nearly threadbare. She wondered if Douglas Abbot was as wealthy as she'd been led to believe. If so, why hadn't he replaced the rug?

She went into the familiar dining room where the wedding meal had been served and looked more closely at the pictures on the walls. There was one of a bucolic scene with horses and cattle and a large barn in the background. The painted portrait was of a family: a man, a woman and three girls; and she knew it was Douglas and his wife and the girls when they were younger. Abby was no more than a babe in her mother's arms.

They looked happy; smiling and gay. She turned away.

She had no picture of Jeffrey except one taken in his uniform before he left for battle. There'd never be a family portrait like this one. She went from the dining room into the kitchen and opened doors and drawers and recognized some of the current patterns of dishes and the usual complement of pots, pans and skillets. She moved on to a side room and saw that it was a study or office. It was plainly male in appearance, with bookshelves and a desk with a leather-bound chair behind it. She took a book from a shelf and read the title, which sounded intriguing. She put it on the desk, thinking to read it soon.

She heard a sound and turned.

"I see you've found my favorite room. Do you like to read?" He pointed to the book, and she nodded, suddenly shy before him. He blinked at the colorful dress she wore. "You'll find mostly history and agriculture with a few dull religious tomes about." He looked around as if seeing the room for the first time. "My wife hated to read. She thought it a waste of time. There are some women's magazines around somewhere, I suppose. My aunt was fond of looking through the fashion books and patterns. Please sit down. The older girls are doing their lessons, and Abby has gone to sleep, worn out by all the exercise. They were up very early this morning." He waited until Maddie was seated in a cloth-bound chair near the desk and seated himself in a matching one beside her.

"I didn't see your aunt today. Is she away on a trip? I'd like to have made her acquaintance." Maddie watched as a flush appeared on his face and his ears turned red.

"I'm afraid you won't be meeting her in the future. She's abandoned us. She said that since I've remarried, she needn't stay, and she left on the early morning train. That's why the girls were up early." He sighed and turned away, gazing out the window with a sad look in his eyes.

"Your eyes are blue; I thought them gray. And, your hair curls on top. Did your wife have blonde hair? I only vaguely remember her, but I saw the picture in the dining room. She was lovely. Sally and Abby take after her, but Nellie has your looks. I hope they'll grow to like me. I'm sorry that Sally saw us earlier, for it made her sad." Maddie realized that she was chattering and stopped in embarrassment, in case he thought her too personal in her observations.

"No, don't apologize. It's better that the girls grow accustomed to seeing us together, for I intend to cuddle and kiss you when I please." He looked at her with a gleam in his eyes, and she rose and sat in his lap. "That is, if you agree to it, too."

She ran her hand through his hair, and he laughed. He dropped his hand to her lap, and with anticipation, his lips touched hers in a passionate embrace. She responded with equal passion, and he pulled away in dismay at her unexpected fervor.

"How many? How many men have you taken into your arms since your husband left, for I can't believe after that display that I'm the first." Douglas removed her from his lap and stood with his hands stiff at his sides, and his face reflected puzzlement and disgust. A feeling of shock surged through her, and she drew herself up in defense.

"You, sir, are the first. Whether you believe me or not doesn't matter. I didn't want this marriage. I was forced into it by my mother and older brother, and by the hand and cruel words of the preacher, Mr. Kitsfield. But, I've made a commitment today, in word and deed. I'll keep my vows. I'll work hard to gain your trust and your respect. Other than that, I can't manage. I'll continue to grieve for my husband, but you are now the lord and master of my destiny. If you wish me to leave your house, you have only to say it, and I'll go."

Maddie searched his eyes for a few more minutes, and not seeing his expression change, with resignation, turned and left the room.

— 3 —

An uneasy silence fell over the household. Douglas changed his clothes and went to the barn for his evening chores. He felt tired and ashamed. He shouldn't have accused her of infidelity. He knew it was wrong. He stayed as long as he could but had to see that his daughters were alright, so he returned to the house, carrying the milk and the eggs from the nests.

Maddie was at the stove, standing relaxed and smiling at the two younger girls who were whispering secrets to each other. Abby was giggling as only a small child can. Sally sat at the table with a book, reading her lesson for the next day of school. She didn't smile at him. Abby jumped up and ran to him as she usually did and threw her small arms around his legs, almost tripping him. Nellie followed somewhat more shyly. He hugged them both.

"Hello, angels. Did you have a nice sleep? Sally, why

don't you put that book away and tell me what you read today."

It was a daily ritual, one that he enjoyed, but the girl refused to obey. She ran from the room and up the stairs. Douglas saw the surprise in his new wife's eyes. With a sigh, and for a distraction, he turned to the milk, strained it and put it in the cellar. He took the morning's pitcher and brought it into the kitchen. The girls had begun chattering, and Maddie listened and made a comment, but Douglas was too worried about Sally's response to hear the words.

He cleaned the eggs and put them away.

Except for the voices of the girls, the room was quiet. A clock ticked and tocked in the hallway with a muted sound, and the chimes tolled the hour. Maddie set the food on the table and helped Abby cut her meat. She poured milk for the girls and coffee for herself and Douglas. She ate without appetite, exhausted from the turmoil and emotions of the day. Douglas led the girls upstairs and helped them get ready for bed. He kissed his younger daughters goodnight and left them to whisper until they fell asleep. Abby wasn't ready to sleep because of her long afternoon nap, but he didn't chastise her for keeping Nellie awake.

He went to Sally's room and found her crying. He soothed her tears and listened to her complaints but was resolute in his decision. She must adjust to the new situation. Aunt Cornelia was gone and wouldn't return. She must learn to accept her new mother and show her respect and obey her. He stayed until she fell asleep, his heart filled with compassion. He walked slowly downstairs, heard the rattle of dishes and knew that Maddie was cleaning up from their meal. He went into the office and was assaulted by the memory of the scene from that afternoon and his shameful part in it.

Not even married twelve hours, and already he had sewn discord between himself and his wife. He sat behind his desk and picked up some letters that needed his attention, but he couldn't concentrate. Would she sleep in his bed tonight? Or, would she find the guest bedroom and choose to sleep alone? He sat still and listened until the kitchen sounds ended and he heard her walk up the stairs. He covered his face with his hands and wept for the peace and tranquility that seemed to elude him. He remembered what she had said about being forced into the marriage and was puzzled. The preacher had assured him that she would welcome the comfort and security of her own home and a father for her child.

Maddie, finished in the kitchen, found herself upstairs in the large bedroom. She hadn't yet unpacked. Her trunk and carpetbag and boxes were still as her brothers had left them. The only change from the afternoon was the black mourning dress tossed over the side of the trunk. She lifted it and pressed it to her body. She remembered the argument with her mother over wearing it to the wedding. Why had she been so adamant? She ran her hand over the soft, satiny cloth but hated the color. She wouldn't wear it again. She tossed it back over the trunk, went to the carpetbag and withdrew a soft flannel nightgown.

She washed herself all over and put it on, letting the folds fall over the rounded proof of her pregnancy. She released her hair from their pins and braid. She placed the pins carefully on the table, for they were a precious commodity, with the war blockades. She brushed her hair until it shone with life and vitality. She left it free, pulled back the covers and climbed into her husband's bed. She smelled the scent of his hair tonic on his pillow. She turned to blow out the candle and saw the picture of his wife on the wall. She snuffed out the light and tried to relax. The picture haunted her. Was this the way he must feel about Jeffry Talley, that someone was standing between them? Well, no longer. She would take whatever he offered, whether large or small, and give what she could in return.

She heard the footsteps on the stairs and listened while he checked the girls' rooms. Everything was quiet and still in the house. She thought she heard the tick of the clock in the hallway near the parlor but decided it was too far away. Perhaps there was another one in the house. She caught her breath when he opened the door and came in. His boots landed with a thump. She heard the rustle of his clothes being removed and falling to the floor. He raised the covers and slid in beside her. He turned and took her in his arms, and she responded with passion and ardor. The bedsprings squealed in protest, but neither of them heard the sound. He bumped his head against the headboard and laughed out loud. Long into the night they discovered the delights of each other's form and secret places.

— 4 —

"Papa, I'm thirsty." Abby's small voice shyly spoke in a whisper, slowly bringing Douglas awake.

He opened one eye and saw his daughter's face, looking like an angel, peering into his. She had soft black hair and a round full face, and he smiled.

"What, Abby? Are you awake so soon? Go back to your room, and I'll be there in a minute, darling."

The tiny girl in the soft blue gown left the room, her eyes wide and puzzled. For the first time she could remember, there was a woman in her papa's bed. She tiptoed to Sally's room and shook her awake.

"Sally, that woman's in Papa's bed. I want a drink of water."

Sally sat up and took the small girl into her arms. Ordinarily soft hearted and compassionate, she held her tight for a moment and then rose and pulled her night robe over herself. Barefoot, she led the other girl down to the toilet and entered the kitchen and gave her a drink of water.

"Abby, she's our mother now, because our first mother went to live with the angels. Remember Papa told us? Mamas and papas sleep in the same bed every night."

"No. Aunt Cornelia and Papa." She shook her head and climbed onto her favorite chair. "I'm hungry." She turned when she heard a sound at the door.

"Here are my girls. I told you, my dear, that we'd find them in the kitchen." Douglas gathered first Abby and then Sally into his arms and smothered them with kisses.

Maddie still wore her flannel gown from the night before, and her face was red with embarrassment each time she glanced at him. Douglas was in a pair of pants, with his nightshirt loosely tucked in the waistband. He smiled each time he caught sight of her, moving as awkwardly as a boy with a first love.

"It's chill in here," Douglas said, finally breaking the silence.

"I suppose we'll need a fire for breakfast." Maddie let out a giggle before putting her hand over her lips to hide her smile.

"You're right, I suppose." Douglas moved to the stove to prepare it for the morning.

While he started the fire, she collected a bowl, a large spoon and a baking pan and set them on the table. Going back to the larder for the flour, lard and tin of soda, she yawned and covered her mouth, her eyes sleepy in her pale face.

Douglas turned and smiled, placed two more sticks into the firebox and filled the coffee pot with water from the keg by the door. He took the coffee grinder from the shelf and opened the bag of coffee beans, took a handful from the bag, and he ground the beans, poured them in the pot and started the pot to perking on the stove. Without a word said, he went to the root cellar and brought out a basket of yesterday's eggs and a portion of a ham hock to the table and began to carve slices from the meat.

Maddie made the batter for biscuits and turned the dough onto a floured board. She got a certain satisfaction from thumping the dough and rolling it across the smooth surface. She sprinkled more flour onto the dough and thumped it again. She shaped twelve thick mounds, placed them in the greased pan and slipped it in the oven.

She knew where the utensils were after last night's meal, so she brought out a good-sized skillet, and she started some eggs to cook. She listened as Douglas took in his daughters' stories and laughed at their gestures and flying hands. Nellie soon joined them, and Douglas left the meat and took them upstairs and helped them dress: the two eldest for school and Abby for her day at home with her new step-mother, leaving Maddie to finish carving the meat and place the slices in a large iron skillet to cook. Steam rose from the ham, and it sizzled in the pan.

As she was peeking into the oven to see how the biscuits were coming along, her husband returned with his daughters, who stopped and gazed with wonder at the sight of the woman in the kitchen. Douglas seated his girls and gave them glasses of water from the pump. Sally, the eldest, had puffy red eyes from her night of crying. She glared at Maddie with sharp intelligent eyes. She was dressed in a pale-yellow dress, her hair neatly braided and pinned on top of her head.

Nellie was a blonde with long red ribbons in her hair; and her eyes a pure blue. She wore a red gingham dress with ruffles around the neck and sleeves.

The youngest child, Abby, pouted and picked up a spoon and tapped the table. "I don't like eggs. I want Aunt Nealie." Her dark curls danced as she shook her head.

Douglas took the spoon from her and looked gently into her eyes. "Your aunt Cornelia has gone to visit her relatives in Kingsborough. She misses her great-niece, and besides, she knew you would want to get to know your new mother. How's that, my little pumpkin?" He smiled at her, trying to get her to laugh.

Maddie continued to stir the scrambled eggs in the skillet and turned the ham slices, pretending that she didn't hear the commotion going on at the table. She checked her biscuits, and taking a thick cloth from the peg beside the stove, brought the pan to the table, releasing a warm, fragrant smell of fresh bread. She dipped the eggs from the skillet into a bowl, brought it to the table and turned back for the ham slices.

Trying to ignore the heat from the cook stove, she brushed a damp spot from her face with the cloth and poured a cup of coffee for Douglas. He quickly finished his meal and went out to milk the cow and feed the chickens and the hogs. He brought in the milk, strained it to remove any dirt particles or insects and went to the corral to hitch the horse to the surrey to drive his older daughters to school. He smiled at his wife and daughters, and for the first time in years, felt true joy in his heart.

When the family had finished eating and left the

kitchen, Maddie cleared the table and began to wash the dishes, with young Abby watching her every move with enormous, curious eyes.

— 5 —

It had been a busy day, and Maddie was tired. Her back ached, and her feet were swollen, so she sat in the parlor to rest. She looked around her and observed that the room seemed stark and bare. There were a few books on a shelf and a pretty lamp on the table in front of the window, but there were no curtains, no pictures on the walls, no lace scarves on the chairs or tables. That was odd, since her mother had said that her husband was a wealthy man. And, why was he doing his own farm chores?

Her mother and siblings lived on a small pension from her father, but even they had two servants.

She rose and walked around the room, touching an item here, pulling a book from the shelf and then replacing it. Puzzled, she decided to ask him. She went down the hallway to his office and, without a warning, walked into the room.

Douglas sat hunched over his desk, writing in a ledger book. She walked up to him, and he looked up in surprise.

"Why do you work so hard?" she demanded. "If you're wealthy, why don't you have hired hands to help you?" She put her hands on her hips and gazed at him aggressively.

"What? Who told you I was wealthy?"

She backed a few steps and frowned. "The preacher and my mother," she said. "Mother said that you needed a wife and mother for your children; that you were very wealthy."

He sighed and put away his papers in a drawer. He pressed the cork into his ink bottle and set it aside.

"Please sit down, my dear. I suppose, to some people, I might seem to be wealthy. I have hundreds of acres of land, but it's mostly forest and uncultivated. The only area cleared off for use is the fifty acres you can see around you. There's the house, the barn, the garden and fields of corn and tobacco. The tobacco's mostly for a cash crop when I need some extra funds. I have several town lots on which I see buildings or houses for the new settlers; I hope to build and profit from them after the war."

"You have no money? My mother said she was receiving a bride price."

"I've some money in the bank, but I'm not wealthy, by any means. I had two hired hands before the war; but they went off to join the army, and I didn't attempt to hire more men. I don't believe in slavery, so that wasn't an option."

"Oh, but why would they say such a thing?"

"Tell me what they said."

She went into a rambling, almost shy explanation of

what the preacher had told her mother about him; and what her mother had demanded of her. She ducked her head in embarrassment. She wrung her hands and looked at the bare boards on the floor.

"My dear girl, I fear you've been deceived." He sat back in his chair and looked at her with dismay. "In fact, your father was one of the wealthiest men in town. It's your mother who's wealthy. Did she never tell you? Your father was a lawyer, correct?"

"Yes."

"And, your older brother's studying with Judge Bartholomew to become a lawyer?"

"Yes."

"When the Rev. Kitsfield approached me about the marriage, I was reluctant at first. I'd grown quite comfortable with the situation as it was; with my daughters, and my aunt to see to their needs. Your mother offered me a large dowry, but I told Judge Bartholomew that I had no need for the funds, but I did need a mother for my daughters."

Maddie gazed at him a moment, then she began to laugh. She almost bent over in her shock and amazement at his droll assessment of her mother's actions. She felt a pain in her belly and sobered up. She wiped the tears from her eyes and rubbed her rounded stomach.

"Are you well?"

"Quite so. I can see that my mother's been very clever, even bold. I've never known her to be so manipulative. But, then, she has other children to settle and will soon find husbands for my sisters Janie and Elizabeth, as well. She's already eighteen years, you know."

48

"You're not angry, or displeased?"

"No, I'm very satisfied if you're pleased with me." She gazed up with a mischievous sparkle in her eyes. She rose and gathered him into her arms.

Douglas hesitated then drew her closer; and he whispered in her ear, "I'm very pleased."

They half stumbled, half walked to the bedroom, and he closed the door tightly behind them.

— 6 —

The back door slammed shut behind Maddie as she left the house.

The two smaller girls ran with abandon toward the chicken coops. Maddie headed first to the shed, where she filled a bowl with corn to scatter for the chickens. When she came out, Nellie was climbing the fence around the pig pen. The ground was damp from the rain the night before, and Maddie called to the child to watch her hold on the fence and to not slip.

"I'll be careful," she called, without turning or seeming to notice what warning was given.

Maddie watched her for a time, smiling at the child's enthusiasm, then she went into the coop to collect the eggs. The dim light made it hard to see until her eyes adjusted, and she breathed in the hay and chicken smell. It was warm and comforting, although she wouldn't have thought so just months ago. One large, red hen walked by her, clucking, telling her to move aside, so she could make her way out the door.

"Excuse me, Miss Polly. I see you've done your duty today." In the nest just vacated by the big hen, a white egg gleamed in the fading light. A child's voice called out in a startled tone, and Maddie turned to the coop door to listen.

Splat! The sound carried into the coop, and Maddie set her basket down and made her way outside as quickly as possible. She found Nellie in the pig pen where she'd fallen, and she was covered with mud. Abby, with a surprised look on her face, ran screaming towards the house.

The sound of his daughter's yells drew Douglas from the barn, carrying the pitchfork in his hand. It bristled with bits of soiled hay from mucking the cow's stall. He stomped across the yard, found his wife with Nellie and rushed into the house after Abby.

Maddie picked up Nellie and visited the horse trough, where she efficiently drew a pail of water and began to clean the girl's face and hands. The dress, however, was hopelessly ruined. She marched her into the house and into the warm kitchen and was confronted by an angry man, his face red with his words.

"Can't you watch the girls better? I trusted you to take care of them."

Maddie ignored him as she stripped Nellie's dress off and sent her upstairs to change into a clean frock. The girl ran upstairs to her sister and was soon followed by Abby, her eyes now dry and her face streaked with her tears. She peeped over the side of the rail at her father as he tried to calm himself.

Maddie drew more water from the pump and tried to clean the dress before it was permanently stained.

"So, Wife, what do you have to say for yourself?" Douglas stood to her side, glaring balefully.

"I . . . I—" She placed one hand on the counter and leaned over, surprised at a twinge in her belly. "I think you should go for a midwife. I suspect my time has come."

"I'll go for Mrs. Upchurch. She's our closest neighbor. You'll be fine until I return?"

"I have no choice. Just go, Douglas."

He saddled his horse, and he was on his way to fetch the midwife.

— 7 —

Betsy Upchurch stayed three days. She was a tall, full-figured, efficient woman of middle age and had five children of her own. Her dresses were limp affairs of brown and gray, in sturdy, coarse fabric, with long sleeves. She favored heavy boots appropriate for the outdoors, although she also wore them inside, telling anyone who asked that they let her wander where she pleased, without the nonsense of having to change. She lived with her husband Nicholas and his younger brother, Hiram. During the three days Maddie was confined to her bed, Nicholas and Hiram came to help Douglas harvest the garden vegetables: onions, potatoes, carrots, squash, beans, beets and turnips.

While the men were working in the garden, Betsy's daughter Clemma, with her long, braided hair and pressed, neat dresses of cotton and linen, watched over the girls, playing with them and continuing their lessons when she could keep them settled down. She could be heard singing to them at night to lull them to sleep.

They named the boy William Anthony Talley Abbot. Douglas made his way to the barn and pulled down the old cradle he and his wife had used for his daughters. It would serve fine for the boy, he shared with Mrs. Upchurch. She agreed, and he took it to the yard with a bucket of water and began to scrub it until the wood shone.

Mrs. Upchurch noticed that Maddie hadn't gathered many clothes or nappies for the baby, and it bothered her. She knew several ladies in town who had recently had children, and in particular Francis Fulham, a cheerful woman whose husband sat on the town council. She instructed Douglas on where to go to get what his wife needed. She suggested he stop by and ask Mrs. Fulham's advice while he was in town.

He arose early on Saturday morning to finish his chores before he drove in for supplies. The thought of baby clothes completely left his mind, however, when he drove near the blacksmith's shop at the edge of town, for the streets were swarming with Union soldiers and horses. He parked the wagon near the smithy's open shop and jumped down and tied the reins to a post.

James Mindell, the blacksmith and farrier, was standing at his anvil and stopped working when he saw Douglas drive up. He was a big man in a leather apron, with thick black hair underneath a leather cap. His trousers were stained with blacking, and one leg had a hole burnt through. His dark, woolen shirt was rolled at the cuffs, exposing arms curled with coarse hair. He left his fire and billows and came to stand with him, as they gazed with wonder at the soldiers.

"What do you think's going on, James?" Douglas removed his hat and wiped his brow with a handkerchief from his back pocket.

"Rumors floatin' about that a large encampment of Confederates been seen about fifty miles from Gettysburg, and the general's preparing for a battle soon."

"A battle? But, why would the Confederates come so far north? Surely not to confiscate our munitions factories or proselytize slave owners around here."

"Don't know the answer, Douglas. Heard it from Ralston in the saloon last night."

"Is that so?" Douglas pursed his lips, pondering the source of the gossip.

"Hear tell they might be encamped round here before too many weeks, if food runs short. A few been seen on the train. Hope that don't cause no trouble for us in these parts." The big man nodded his head and looked at Douglas from under heavy brows.

"You got anything except gossip to share, James?"

"Harrumph! I plan to mind my own business and not ask questions, and I'd advise you to do the same." The blacksmith moved toward his anvil and left Douglas standing in the dust of the street.

Douglas moved on down the street, taking care not to disturb any soldiers in his path. He made his way to the Fulham home, and Fanny gave him a list of clothing and things that Maddie would need for the baby. She handed him some used clothing that her son had overgrown. He thanked her kindly and walked to the post office for his mail. All around him, conversation was buzzing about the upcoming battle, but he kept to his own business as the blacksmith had advised. He was given two letters and put them in his coat pocket, and crossed to Macardle's store where the proprietor, Jake Higgins, filled a wooden box with supplies and seemed ready to gossip about the soldiers. He wiped his countertop with a damp cloth.

"Douglas, Ralston and Cleever said Lee's troops have moved into Maryland. You best keep your rifle handy, out on the farm."

"I'm sorry, Jake. Heard about that from James from the saloon last night. Can't spend an overly amount of time visiting. I can't leave my family alone for long."

Jake glanced out at the solders, and he agreed that it wasn't wise. Douglas walked to his wagon, placed the box and his packages in the back of the wagon, untied the reins and drove away.

At the farm, Douglas only mentioned the soldiers casually, having forgotten his first rush of emotion. Maddie was immediately distraught, although he assured her there would be no battles that would affect them. The soldiers were bivouacked in the fields about twenty miles northwest of the town. She worried that the girls would be frightened by the sounds of the cannon, and Douglas assured her it was only a slim possibility. He showed her the letters, opened them and offered to read them to her, if she wished.

They were both from his aunt Cornelia, and she declined, remembering the circumstances in which she'd abandoned the family. The first letter advised him that she had arrived safely and was pleased with her new home. But, the second letter was filled with complaints and dissatisfaction with her new situation. He shook his head and put the letters away in a drawer. Even if his aunt was able to return, it wasn't safe with a future battle pending.

He didn't say anything of his aunt's possible travel back to the farm. It might not happen, and it would be time to deal with it then, if required.

— 8 —

As the weeks and months passed, the couple began to open up more about their previous spouses, and Maddie discovered that his first marriage had been unhappy, filled with arguments and frustrated love. She wasn't surprised when the picture disappeared from their bedroom and reappeared in Sally's room, but she insisted he keep the family portrait in the dining room, for the girls should know their mother.

She told him of her mother's dominance and her siblings' rivalry for affection. In small snippets, Douglas learned each of their characters as seen through his wife's eyes, often looking at her askance when she described some of their wilder antics. It became a tease for him, insisting she prove her stories to be fact rather than fancy, which she did with great detail.

Douglas visited the encampment of soldiers that had

formed across the river, in hopes he could sell some livestock for cash money. He hadn't realized the cost of two extra mouths to feed, and if there was enough, Maddie had expressed a wish to attend her brother's graduation from medical school.

The men had muddied the fields with their boots, due to regular exercise formations and practice with their weapons. A dozen or so tents were set up near some trees, and along the bottom edges, the canvas was stained with mud. Lines stretched to the sides, anchoring the poles and creating hazardous conditions for nighttime strolls, it seemed to Douglas. To one side, a cook's wagon belched smoke into the air. A long sideboard stretched across wooden horses, for preparing food and for the men to eat. The aroma of beans and collard greens was less than appetizing, but the soldiers were surely used to it.

Inside a large tent with the end pulled wide, a table of men in army boots, trousers and shirts were playing a card game. The tent had a plank floor, unevenly laid but dry. To the back were two cots, neatly made, with a trunk at the foot of each one. A dog lay curled on the floor. He lifted his head and barked listlessly when Douglas rode by.

One of the men called to him, "Stranger! Welcome to Creekside Army Camp. Have you any money in your satchel?"

The men with him laughed overly loud, and Douglas could see bottles of drink sitting around. Gaming pieces were scattered across the table, with paper bills held down with stones.

His interest was aroused, and he called, "Some. You got any I can abscond off you? My accounts have been doing poorly, and they could use a little refreshment from your deep pockets."

"That's an attitude I like. Come in, stranger, and share your name."

Before the card game was over, while Douglas had lost as many hands as he won, he'd struck up a deal for grain and a herd of farm animals to be delivered to the camp by the end of the week. He left satisfied, knowing he'd lined his pocket with more funds than which they'd lined theirs.

He stopped by town on the way back to the farm, went to the post office to see what might have come in, and purchased a sack of refined sugar at the general store. From the post office, he slipped a merchandise catalogue for household goods into the bag with the sugar, confident Maddie would enjoy dreaming, even if much of it was far too expensive for their farm's budget. Still, when the deal from the army camp was concluded, perhaps there would be something she could buy.

A fight erupted just as he passed the saloon. Crackers Ridgeon came crashing through the doors and landed in an especially large wagon rut. His black, wool trousers were filthy with the street, and his shirt was only partially tucked under his suspenders. His dark-gray shirt boasted patched sleeves, with a hole in the tail that drooped out the back. Douglas' horse reared at the sudden disruption, nearly sending his conveyance sideways.

"Crackers, man, what the hell?"

"Keep out of this, Abbot. You get back to your farm where you belong." Ridgeon struggled to his knees, and he began to roll his sleeves. Inside the saloon, the crack of wood told of more going on.

"Let me help you out of the street, at least." Douglas pulled his horse up, secured the reins, and leaped to the ground. He took Ridgeon's arm to help him stand.

"Thanks. I got me a fight going on." Ridgeon grinned, stumbling up the steps and through the door.

Douglas scowled and tramped after him. He peered in the doorway, once moving aside when a local by the name of Mortimer Fousheimer fell through, before stumbling back inside. By the time the fight was over, multiple refreshments had been shared, and Douglas was several coins lighter for his visit. He shared the tale with Maddie, who warned him that the place would do no man any good. Douglas laughed and said it had never done him any harm.

Samuel Foster came to visit the farm and enjoyed his stay. He discovered being a farmer wasn't so bad, especially when Douglas offered to help him out of a delicate situation he had fallen into with a certain young lady of his acquaintance. The two men spent one afternoon visiting the saloon of ill repute, where Sammie learned the fun-loving side of his farmer brother-in-law. They joined in a card game, losing only so much as they had in their pockets before abandoning the game and heading out the door, after a final round at the bar.

Sammie insisted Douglas let him see the location of the army camp. The men observed it from the far embankment of the river, with Douglas pointing out the officers' tents. Several soldiers were bare-chested and chasing each other in a game involving a rudely sewn cloth ball. After a time, Sammie and Douglas tired of watching and turned their horses towards the farm.

The two men had a thoughtful discussion around the

fire that evening about the original settlers of the area.

"Quakers, weren't they, Douglas? I understand they decry violence, then manufacture munitions that supply the war."

"That I can't answer, my young friend." Douglas shook his head. Their conversation continued about the activities they'd observed at the army camp, as the fire burned into the night. The hour was late when the lamps were extinguished, and tired eyes and exhausted minds found their way to bed. Sammie returned to school pleased that the marriage was going well.

On his first visit, Johnnie remarked on the baby that had been born, a boy with almost no hair and a loud bellow if not fed when he demanded it. On his second visit, Johnnie and the other family members roamed the fields on horseback. By the time John William Foster had joined the law firm of Judge Mathias Bartholomew, he'd mellowed somewhat from his previous stiff, pompous manner. He indulged his young nieces with a treat at the local ice cream parlor and took them riding in his fine, yellow-wheeled carriage pulled by matching black stallions.

Elizabeth Foster married a merchant in the town, Paulus Browning, and was blessed with one child, a girl named Anne. Jane Foster became a nurse at Johnstown General Hospital and married a doctor, Theodore Glencannon. They worked tirelessly with the wounded and dying veterans of the war.

Douglas and Maddie received an invitation to Samuel's graduation from the Washington Medical College of Baltimore, but with the local rumors and newspaper accounts growing stronger each week, telling of horrible battles, Douglas couldn't chance taking Maddie and the infant on the train so far from home.

Life on the farm continued at a steady pace. Elsewhere, Frankie Wilcox remained single and rumors flew like a grass fire when she moved in with Gertrude Justine. Walindra Foster married at the age of fifty-five to Wallace Griffith, whom she had known for quite some time.

— 9 —

The fall and winter had been fruitful, with fall vegetables and fruits harvested, and over forty pies cooked and stored in the attic, including various berries, pumpkin, squash, mincemeat and several custards. The cellar bulged with salt-cured hams wrapped in canvas and bacon slabs in cheesecloth, stored alongside tins of spices, barrels of flour and bags of coffee beans.

In February, Douglas received another letter from his aunt Cornelia complaining and begging him to send for her. He was troubled by the message but wrote a polite letter back telling her he thought it would be too dangerous for her to travel with the turbulence of war and the uncertainty of the future.

He received no reply.

Maddie was in full bloom, and her skin glowed with the rigors of the winter season. A new colt kicked up in the corral, and the chickens had begun laying in earnest, providing very nearly more eggs than they could eat. The black and white pigs spent much of their time in the barn, oinking hungrily when the slops were brought their way.

The weekly newspapers, when they got them, were filled with news of battles, and the list of the dead mounted in the square: Matt Tuttle, Neal Howard, the widow Jackson's son, Abner, and Woodrow Stone.

On the farm, life seemed insulated from the horrors of the war. The days had been tranquil and content, with nothing to remind them that the country was in danger of being torn apart. Douglas was in the corral with one of the horses, who seemed to be breathing heavily. He felt along its flank and then the underbelly but could find nothing to alarm him. Suddenly, from the direction of town, he heard a great crash, and then smoke began to rise in a gray cloud, seen above the treetops near the river.

He ran into the house, took his rifle from the pegs above the fireplace and told Maddie he was going to investigate. Not giving her time to answer, he flung himself aboard the brown stallion, riding without a saddle, and headed toward town.

As he came closer to the railroad tracks and the scene of the carnage, he could smell burning human flesh, smoke and leaking oil from the train engine, which was overturned in the shallow riverbed. Metal was sheared from one side, exposing the workings of the apparatus. Steam hissed fitfully, indicating the fire in the box wasn't completely extinguished. One train car, with its red-and-black striping scoured by the fall, was on the bank, and another dangled precariously on the edge of the trestle and looked to fall over at any moment. Broken glass littered the riverbank, and it glittered in the sun. The suspended car's metal wheels screeched fitfully with each swaying gust of wind or movement by those inside. Frantic men were trying to get the passengers out of the dangling car before it rolled off the rails, causing it to tip fitfully each time anyone moved any distance at all.

Douglas jumped from his horse, tied the reins to a tree limb safely back from the wreckage and slid down the gravel embankment to join the men working with the passengers. The screams of the women rang in his ears, and he winced. Noah Sanders half lifted, half carried a small boy from the train car's broken window and handed him to Douglas, who then gave him to Ned Bounder, who laid him on the soft grass.

Another child was lifted from the window, and Douglas soon lost count of the people he helped that day. As the last of the passengers was carefully lifted from the window, a great creaking sound arose, and the men jumped to safety as the car shifted its weight. With a powerful groan, the great beast rolled down the embankment to join its twin at the edge of the water.

Douglas stared in dismay and then helped Noah to his feet. Overhead, the clouds had started to build, as though angry at the damage done to the lushness of the green and fertile landscape.

"Thank you, Douglas. We didn't save the luggage, but no people were aboard." Noah wiped his hands on his trousers, leaving muddy streaks. One shoe was half off, and he kicked his foot into the soil to wedge it back on his foot. His face was smeared the color of the dirt, and there was a cut on his forehead.

"You're injured." Douglas nodded toward the gash. He grinned with the relief of the moment. "Worse than many of those riding in the train, I think."

Noah wiped his head with his arm, saw the blood and dismissed it with a puff of his cheeks. He clapped his hands together and nodded his head in a decision.

"We should examine the next car. I suspect that before long, the fire we see at the engine will spread to the woods if it's not tamped down soon."

His answer was a crack of thunder, and rain began to fall. The rescued passengers scrambled for the protection of several nearby trees, with the woman pulling up their hems to run as quickly as the wet grass would allow. Three Union soldiers riding on the train offered them their aid, and with each other's help, they soon made it to the limited safety of the trees.

There was one passenger car, the mail car and the caboose still on the tracks, undamaged, while the engine and two passenger cars, one atop the other, lay twisted, with collapsed roofs and broken windows on the river bank. The conductor was examining the tracks to be certain of their condition. Noah and Douglas joined him, and he pronounced them secure. He pointed at several logs that had joined the engine on its way down the riverbank, determining them the cause of the wreck.

A tall, burley man wearing a dark blue uniform and brass railway insignia on his cap joined them. "Probably a treacherous act by one of the army groups, to thwart supplies being delivered to an enemy camp."

There was a general consent that he was probably correct when Noah looked down the embankment and gave a shout of alarm.

The fire had indeed gone up from the engine and had begun spreading to the nearby forest. The soldiers from before had formed a bucket line of sorts, using what they could find to hold water. Noah was of the opinion it would soon be out, as the rain had increased. Douglas left them, went to his horse, and rode home, his part in the operation finished.

The official report printed in the newspapers would reveal six dead, including the Rev. Mr. Kitsfield, who was discovered to be a Confederate spy. He was traveling with his lover, who was uninjured and disappeared in the confusion. One soldier from the Union Army was burned to death; a civilian merchant traveling from Pittsburg, Willard Bentley, and his wife, Jerusha, were found crushed in the same seat; and a child that Douglas had helped rescue from the passenger car had a pierced lung and succumbed to the pain. The engineer was also found dead, having been thrown from the engine.

The twelve that were wounded, none seriously, had fallen with the first car that had rolled into the river and were evacuated.

The blame was given to the Rebel Army, for the mail car contained the military payroll, but it was kept safe by the soldiers who were riding aboard.

— 10 —

Upon arriving at the farm, with his clothes filthy, his muscles sore and his sense of the world shattered, Douglas paused at the back step and looked to the gray skies and the gently falling rain. He went to the kitchen and pumped some water into a pan, removed his shirt and washed his face, neck and hands. He donned a fresh shirt and tucked the tail into his trousers. The house was quiet, and his footsteps echoed in the hallway.

Two days later, Maddie stood at the window gazing at the new colt cavorting in the barnyard, its mother standing protectively nearby, as Douglas returned from town. Her waist was slim and flat, with no sign she'd borne a child. She wore a clean gingham dress of pale blue. Sally read from a book; the younger two girls were upstairs asleep, as was the baby in his cradle. She watched him disappear into the barn, leading his horse by the reins.

She watched the scene for a time with a melancholy air and sighed. "I hope the war ends soon; but I fear it will last for years." With the soft sound of boots on bare wood, she felt the presence of her husband behind her.

"Maddie, I have some news from the train," he shared, and she turned in his arms.

They talked for an hour, trying to work out how people could be so cruel to one another. Afterward, she sat on the sofa near the window as Douglas wrapped his arm around her and rested his cheek against her hair.

"When, oh, when will it all end?"

"We're safe here, my precious. We've no worries." He gently stroked her hair. "I heard in town Mr. Kitsfield's lover was apprehended. She was working as a saloon girl in Kelbyville. She gave herself away by a locket with his picture and a snip of his hair. You would think she'd run away, being a traitorous spy. Apparently, she was a working girl all along."

"You can't find that amusing." Maddie strained to hide a smile. "She deserves her punishment, though I think being with Mr. Kitsfield was penance enough. Thank you for comforting me, my husband."

"You've not seen your sister for some days. Would she appreciate a visit from you?"

"I could drive the surrey to see Elizabeth about decorations for the upcoming church quilt raffle and social." She smiled, with a pleased expression. "We spoke of it at the church the weekend previous, but Mama was in a hurry to get away, and there's much to be done."

"I'll hitch the horse in the morning, and you can spend the day with happier thoughts. Your sister will be pleased to see you."

He rose and stopped at the fireplace to put another log on the fire, and he glanced at his daughter. "Sally, shouldn't you be in bed?"

She looked up from her book. "Must I? It's early, yet." Just at that moment the clock on the mantle struck nine of the clock, and they all laughed.

Maddie walked to her step-daughter and held out her hand. "Yes, my dear, you must." They walked from the room, and Douglas remained in his chair, gazing at the sparks flying up the chimney. Outside, the dog barked, and he strolled to the back door. He made sure it was firmly secured, placed the fireguard in front of the fireplace, blew out the lamp and yawned. Yes, it was time for his rest. He slowly moved up the stairs and into the room he shared with his wife.

The colt outside neighed and kicked up its hooves, thrilled with life and unconcerned about the scene of destruction near the river.

The Good Fight

— Prologue —

Peter Worsham, a recent law student at the University of Colorado, traveled along Highway 285 out of Denver to visit his fiancée's parents for the first time. He had an important decision to make: whether to take a lucrative position he'd been offered with a law firm in Denver or a lowly job as paralegal and clerk in the District Attorney's Office in Pueblo County. With the latter, he would receive less pay but gain more experience in executing criminal law.

He had studied the decisions and briefs of Judge A. P. Alcott, one of the first district judges in the territory, recommended by his professor and mentor, John Calhoun, during his last semester at the college. Professor Calhoun had pointed him to the newspaper clippings and articles in the library archives about the 1867 case in which Judge Alcott had sent an innocent boy to prison and later found that his own son was the guilty party. The case was The Territory of Colorado vs. Jacob Hale.

After spending weeks researching and thoughtfully writing an essay on the case, Peter decided to make an overnight stop at the Whispering Pines State Park, encompassing the ranch where the innocent man had lived out his life after his release from prison. The park was on his route, and he would enjoy a respite from the grinding last months of study for the bar examination. He loved nature, and fishing was his most passionate way of relaxing.

Peter pulled up to the entrance of the campground and paid his fee. He strolled through the small museum and was intrigued by the pictures and relics of the early settlers to the area, including those from the Hale family ranch. A color portrait of the man who donated the land was hung in a prominent spot near the entrance, and Peter was impressed by photographs of the cowboy astride his horse, Jasper, his face toughened by the outdoor life he led. Stepping outside the side door, he could just see a patch of distant, snow-capped mountains beyond the Ponderosa pine forest for which the park was named. He put a dollar bill in the vending machine and received a cold, damp soft drink. He took a deep swallow and felt the cool, tingling liquid move down his throat.

He looked around him at the picnic tables and the natural rock pavilion and watched a chattering squirrel scamper up a tree. Turning slightly to the right, he located a sign and cast-iron fence perched on the slope above the pavilion and started up the path. He stood a long time outside the fence, gazing at the tall, imposing marker of Jacob Allyson Hale and its epitaph. This, he knew from his research, was the man who had been sent to prison for a crime he didn't commit. He turned away, moved slowly down the path and tossed his empty can into the receptacle. As he gazed once more at the mountains, with their snowy peaks turned pink in the late afternoon sun, Peter's future seemed more clearly defined. It was as if he'd received the answer to his dilemma.

He drove his car to the camping space assigned to him, opened the trunk and took out his fishing equipment. He whistled as he walked to the lake shore. He could hardly wait to tell Lucile and her parents his decision. But, it would have to wait until he caught a big trout for his supper.

As his line created ripples in the water, he thought of how a person's actions in life can cause ever-repeating consequences that affect everyone around him. He considered how the lives of Judge Alcott and Jacob Hale had intertwined and overlapped, until the affectionate bond that grew between the two former antagonists had resulted not only in Hale's own knowledge of the law on the American frontier, but in this peaceful, scenic oasis preserved for future generations. As he sat on the shore and pondered the matter, Peter pictured the events as they might have happened a century and a half before . . .

— 1 —

The heavy iron prison gates, stained black with years of confiscated and pummeled dreams, clanged shut behind the young man, a gunshot ricochet echoing in his ears. Relief forced the hairs on his arms erect as his skin prickled, even as dread ate at his stomach. His childhood friend was dead, though how much of a friend he had been was a knob of stone in his stomach. The dust swirled around his feet, a tornado of life he wasn't sure he wanted, and he stood for a moment, the echo of sound loud in his ears. Tall and slender, he ran a wide hand across his scalp. Before crossing through those gates the first time, his dark hair had curled around his ears, long and carefree. Today, it was clipped short and high, a prickly brown lawn covering his scalp.

Jacob Allyson Hale was twenty-two years old.

He drew in a deep breath and walked along the roadway leading to the town, shuffling his feet as though the iron chains still dragged from his ankles. Hard and bright memories of his time on the other side of those gates buzzed like bees in his head, threatening to alight and raise painful whelps at any moment. A cough caught in his throat, the dust from the unpaved road rising to wrap his legs at each step, and some of it reaching skyward to dart into his lungs at every breath. The creases in his dark trousers were magnets. The hems soon looked closer to the color of the soil than the material from which they were woven. Occasionally, he brushed the toe of one shoe against the back of his leg, ignoring that he was leaving more dust behind. He couldn't see it, and it was something he had no energy over which to fret. He turned for a moment to look behind him. The heavy walls of the prison blotted out the horizon, as if sucking the very essence of life from the sky. He twisted his tongue in his mouth, balled up a wad of saliva, and flung it at the dirt. He would never darken this cursed soil again. God help him, his life would be different from this day forward, whatever it took for that to be true.

Straightening his back, he began his journey once more, one heavy foot at a time, the soles of his blunt shoes dragging the soil along after him, as if it wanted to escape, also. No one had suggested a ride to him, and if offered, he might have turned it down. A carriage passed him, the rattling of the wooden conveyance creating a staccato rhythm that thumped against the bars of his dark thoughts, and after a glance, he let his eyes fall hard to the dried tracks on the soil just in front of him. He ignored the stares of the occupants, though their curious eyes seemed to bore through his coat. A horseman rushed by on some imagined mission of importance, stirring even more dust than Jacob. Soon, the powdery detritus began to whiten the black shine of his newly purchased shoes quicker than he could wipe them clean, and the brown film eventually covered the lower portion of his dark trousers like icing on a cake.

The suit was a gift of the territory, the shirt boiled and bleached (perhaps having once belonged to another man), with a heavy dreadnaught overcoat, one hundred dollars in gold coin and the blunt shoes. The coat buttons were the color of a biscuit. All released prisoners were given such things to start them on the journey to their home, the warden had told him, along with a lecture on honor and duty and decency of character. The warden had been shocked when the news broke over the telegraph wires that the prisoner, Jacob Hale, with his drizzle of freckles, was innocent of the crime for which he had been sent to prison for ten years. A man had been shucked off from a rail car during a robbery and severely injured. In a delirium of pain and morphine, he had burbled like a river in an endless thunder about various crimes he had foisted upon innocent people. His name was soon put with his person, placing his father as the judge who had passed the sentence in Jacob Hale's case. The judge was appalled to learn he was the father of the real criminal in the series of unfortunate events.

The judge's son, Jonathan Petro Alcott, once Jacob's friend from their childhood, was the focus of a huge investigation after the discovery that he had been thrown like a pig carcass from the railroad car while attempting to rob the train from Garden City. His back was broken, and in the three days during his battle with the dark specter of death, he confessed a string of stage holdups, store robberies and illegally procured gold shipments from the mining town of Denver. The fact that he was the son of the Territorial District Judge who had presided at the trial and sentencing of Jacob Hale became an item of prominent news in the newspapers, from the largest printed rags to the half-sheets in the smaller towns.

As he lay on his bed twisting and fighting his caregivers in the excruciating throes of his imminent demise, Alcott, in his lucid moments, spoke to several witnesses, including his father, of how he had laughed while sitting in his father's courtroom as his friend and schoolyard chum had been tried and sentenced to the penitentiary for his own crime. It had amused him at the time to hear the three passengers describe himself as the bandit, and still no one had suspected him. He made sure from that moment on that his own character in and around the town of Whitesboro was pure and spotless. Other people might live perfectly fine and acceptable with water the color of brick swirling around their feet, but his deeds must be clear as a mountain stream. His invigorating and seemingly impossible escape from the clutches of justice led to a feeling of invincibility, encouraging him to continue his bullying rampage against what was good and proper and part of the law. To all eyes, he was a loyal and dutiful son. His father, the judge, proud of his son's behavior, often compared him to the example of Jacob Hale, who had traveled the path of wicked lawlessness. Now, the tables were turned, and it was the townspeople and the judge who suffered shame and remorse for their treatment of the innocent Jacob, who had been tending his father's cattle, oblivious to the tragedy about to befall him.

After the death and funeral of Jon Alcott (as Jonathan was called since a child), a new trial, in absentia, was begun with a different judge and jury. Townspeople gathered on the raw, new boardwalks in anticipation, women in bonnets with strings tied under their chins, a number wearing new-fashion pancake hats in straw, and the men in cutaways, with high collars and cravats, with side-button black shoes. The sky was washed with clouds, and as freight wagons click-clacked down the rough stone and brick streets, the crowd cheered at the overwhelming judgment of the jury that the prisoner was to be released from his incarceration immediately. One man who was lightly agreeable with drink cleared his throat loudly, a frog croaking against the din of the pond, and cocking his head like a titmouse, he groped in his head for a phrase or a sentence, until he finally let out a Well done! Laughter tittered around him, building like a wind come a-running. It took an additional three months for the final wheels of justice to roll in Jacob's favor, and at last, the wrongly imprisoned young man was released. He walked through the gates of the prison like a colt broken to harness, with a folded piece of paper in his pocket, a free man. What should have been a healing moment like curative waters instead was the feeling of a dipper dropped in a bucket, a hollow clap of metal against liquid, and the quiet clink as it hit the bottom. During the time of his incarceration, Jacob's father had died, still believing in his son's guilt.

Jacob walked to the outskirts of the town and headed straight for the railroad depot, where he purchased a ticket to Whitesboro. He then strode in his shuffling walk to the local saloon, where he took one drink of whiskey and, with a portion of his hundred dollars, visited the room of a young woman upstairs. The events of the evening became shining motes of shifting dandelion seeds following him wherever he walked, obvious in his changed manner and lifted head. Walking from the saloon with a smile of pleasure, he went to the nearest store and bought a pair of work trousers, a couple of twill shirts, other necessary garments, and a pair of leather boots. His one hundred dollars now almost depleted, he waited at the depot until his transportation arrived, a vehicle built of metal and forced to hold the world together bolt by bolt. He boarded the train and, like a ruffled grouse startled by the events of his life, flew on the metal monster to the home of his birth.

— 2 —

The train arrived at the station on time, clickety-clack,
and a young, tall, slender man leaped from the steps with
a lilt that hadn't been there days before. It had been a long
journey. As the train had passed the area near the town, the
snapping of the iron wheels on the tracks singing a taunting
song, he had looked toward the large white house on the
hill, its windows now boarded up with new slats of lumber,
its panes of glass darkened against the world's prying eyes.
The yard was unkempt and overgrown with weeds, like a
tousled boy's head just arising from his pillow. Jacob
would have liked to see more, but the scene flashed past
his window, and he caught a glimpse of the low, sprawling,
unpainted house next door, the home of banker Elias Tammersham. Next, in a flash came the Methodist church with
its cemetery and its parsonage, the Two Pennies a Day
Drug Store, the Truman Simmons General Store (a famil-

iar sight) and the Thompson Livery Stable. The train rolled to a screeching stop with a bellow of pain and a puff of black smoke, as though it had eaten a bad meal and its stomach had soured.

Jacob stood for a moment taking in the changes near the train depot. It was like a postal card with portions of it painted over with new images. He carried his brown satchel containing his few possessions in his left hand and strode forward. With the return to his familiar surroundings, his shuffle was back, and he took a few steps and stopped. He drew in a deep breath, ignoring the smoke from the train, and began to move toward the center of town. He also ignored the dread in the eyes of the few witnesses who watched him with fear. One woman carried a basket with the heads of alarmed chickens protruding. Another held the hand of a child and scurried past. A strange hum began to grow, like bees in a disturbed hive searching for protection from an unnamed aggressor, as people passed the word: Jacob Hale is back.

Jacob continued his journey until he came to the building that held the Law. Above the door, a weathered sign said Sheriff's Office. He strode up the steps, turned the handle and stepped inside. A large, broad-shouldered man turned at his entrance and froze in his steps. The sheriff's deputy, Maximillian Gruggor, stared, the unmistakable look of fear in his eyes. He had never believed Jacob was as innocent as the courts had claimed. His hand started for the gun at his side, a wild thing not under his control, and he stopped, his arm frozen in mid-reach, as if confused whether to draw and shoot or return to what he was doing.

"Hello, Max." The former prisoner stepped forward

and held out his hand. "I guess you know why I've come. Is the sheriff available?"

Max Gruggor ignored the offered hand and stepped back as far as he could, as though the touch of the former resident of the town might contaminate him in some way.

"No, he's gone over to Johnson City, to investigate a burglary there."

"When do you expect him back?" Jacob dropped his hand and stepped back himself. He looked slowly around the office. Nothing seemed to have changed. The papers were still on the desk in a haphazard manner, and the old pot-bellied stove sat in the corner with its blackened coffee pot on the top. The rifles, one a .56 caliber Colt carbine, were lined up in a row in the glass-covered cabinet near the cell block. An Irish tin whistle glinted on a shelf. He shuddered at the thought of his time spent in a back cell and fought to keep the darkness of that time from eating the light from today's sky.

"I expect he'll be back tomorrow, or maybe the next day. Can't say for sure." Gruggor continued to look at Jacob with that same strange gleam, like an alley cat backed into a corner, and Jacob decided to turn him free.

"Well, I'll stay in town until he returns. I'll be at the hotel if I can get a room there. Tell the sheriff I'll be back. Thanks, Max." As he turned to leave, a feeling of relief washed over his body and mind like a storm rolled up in the sky, and the sun breaking through.

"Wait, Jake." The old familiar name slipped out before Gruggor could stop it from leaving his mouth.

"Yes?" Jacob turned back, keeping his face a stiff board, as his heart stopped beating. The sound of his name brought back memories of a time when youth's grass was still green, and his wild yearnings had yet to be clipped.

"I don't know if you are aware that Sue Blandon is now married."

Fresh, hot and painful the memories came back, but Jacob refused to let them show on his face. Sue had been the girl he had danced with that last time he had been free to dance and laugh and play with his friends. He stood in the manner in which he had been taught, while waiting for the warden or one of the guards to pronounce his restrictions or orders. He firmed his back and straightened his shoulders. He unconsciously raised his chin.

"Yes, I know. I was told that she married Tatum Jordon. My father wrote me at the time. What of it?"

The deputy seemed to relax his body a bit. "I just wondered if you knew. The sheriff and me. We don't want any trouble. As long as you behave yourself and come for your monthly visits, we'll let you alone. She's got two kids, too, both boys. Tatum has that small farm on the old road to the Elder's place, you know. Doing alright for himself, I hear."

There was a question in his eyes, and Jacob knew what he was asking.

"You can tell Tatum if you see him that he has no cause to worry. I don't plan to cause any trouble in town. I done had enough of that for a lifetime." And, with a small shrug of the shoulders, Jacob turned and left the sheriff's office.

He looked to the left and right and noticed a small crowd had gathered near Simmons General Store. There were a few more men standing near the livery stable. People wondering about him, he guessed. He paused a few more seconds, watching them, and turned right toward the lawyer, Frank McGee's office. He felt his shuffling stride and tried to lengthen his steps but found it near impossible. He could almost feel the heavy chains on his ankles, like a great man holding to his legs and weighing him down. He pulled them forward as if by sheer will, but they wouldn't prance like a fancy horse pulling a lady's uptown pram. His hands shook. He looked down at the satchel in his left hand and pulled it closer to his body, as though to protect himself from his fears. He had dreaded this first meeting with the sheriff more than he realized. This twice-monthly check-up required by the warden for his provisional release had been the only restriction to his movements. It proved more than anything, even after the witnesses and the death-bed confession of Jonathan Alcott, that the Law wasn't finished with him.

*****

Coming to the entrance of the office of the lawyer Frank McGee, Jacob knocked on the door, turned the handle and walked in. He'd never been in the office of the prosecutor before. His own lawyer had been a drunken sot named Moore, half asleep during the whole trial, but it was the best his father could afford. With the whole town against him, he'd been lucky to have a lawyer at all. Moore was dead now. He had been found in the alley fallen in his own vomit alongside a broken wine bottle. At the recollection, like a chilling winter dervish sweeping down from the mountains, the memory of his own involvement with the evil temptress prickled his skin, and Jacob shuddered at the thought of how many times he had gone home drunk and his father had turned his back on him in disappointment.

Frank McGee, in gartered shirtsleeves and galluses, arose from behind his shined and carved walnut desk, prepared to meet the young man in front of him. He slipped on a cutaway frock, seamlessly and with ease, as he moved forward. The desk was an ostentatious and flamboyant excess that told of the man's personality. He had shared with his contemporaries that he expected to be among the first persons Hale would come to see. Jacob crossed the room and shook the offered hand. The two men gazed at each other, and Jacob could see that same look of awe and fright in the eyes of the lawyer that the deputy had displayed.

"Mr. McGee." He hadn't the courage to say anything more. He used the excuse of dropping his satchel on the floor by the desk to mask his embarrassment.

"Jacob Hale. I see that your experience hasn't changed your looks much. How do you feel? I heard you came on the afternoon train. Have you been to see the sheriff?"

Jacob felt the air thicken, woven with the broken skeins of his life exposed for all to see. The town noises on the other side of the door became no more than the crackling of soil on a sunbaked plain. The man standing in front of him surely knew all the details of his release from prison, a black stain on his young life.

"I feel fine. And, yes, I went to see Sheriff Gomez. He wasn't there, Max Gruggor said. He's gone over to Johnson City on a burglary case. Be back tomorrow or the next day, maybe. I'll stay in town until he returns."

Reassured at the news, McGee relaxed and moved behind his desk to sit down. He pointed to a low-backed, horsehair chair in front of the desk, and Jacob sat down.

He gazed thoughtfully at the former wild boy of the town. Jacob stared back just as intently. He had participated in a few poker games with McGee, Tatum Jordon and Max Gruggor when in town. McGee had also been the main prosecutor at his trial, and he had had a chance to observe the lawyer during the proceedings. The man had thought him guilty, despite their friendship, Jacob knew.

McGee rapped his knuckles on the oiled leather surface of his desk twice then leaned forward with his hands clasped together. He cleared his throat, a short frog-like croak, before speaking in a matter-of-fact tone, as if relating well-established facts before a panel of inquiry. "Judge Alcott felt very guilty after discovering the news of his own son being the robber of the stage coach for which you were sent to prison. He's tried to make amends for the wrong his son and he caused you."

McGee paused to watch the young rancher's face. Jacob sat motionless, focused on the lawyer, his face a blank door. McGee pulled a file from a tray on his desk, and he rubbed one long finger around the beveled edge as though what it contained could only be released by strong incantations and much legalese. He cleared his throat again, a habit, it seemed, and began to speak, his eyes once more on Jacob.

"Besides the investigation that he instigated and the new trial, the judge has left you his property in Whitesboro." Again, the lawyer paused to watch the man's face.

"Property? What do you mean, property? He doesn't owe me anything. I don't want his property." The former convicted criminal was on his feet in protest. His hands shook, and his face turned hot in embarrassment. The surprise and shock of the announcement was a dust devil of disappointment, nay, a swirling tornado of insult, speaking words of superiority over a falsely condemned man old Alcott clearly thought incapable of making a name for himself on his own.

"Sit down, Jake."

Instantly, Jacob found himself in his chair, his hands nervously clasped together, too long accustomed to taking orders. He looked down, surprised that the handcuffs weren't binding his wrists even now. With the sharp words, he had been taken back in an instant. Would he never get over the feeling of the hard steel on his arms? A sense of despair rose to meet this new challenge to his pride. He watched as McGee stood from his chair and walked about the room, gazed without sight at the people gathered in front of the general store in curiosity, then turned back to Jacob.

With a scratching of hard, wooden chair legs on polished plank flooring, McGee lowered himself down, not in the chair behind the desk, but in the identical seat next to his guest. He looked a long time at the folded hands and crossed ankles.

"Jake . . . I hope you don't mind if I call you that. It seems to slip off my tongue as naturally as it did in the old days before the trouble that came between us." Jake shook his head in acceptance of his nickname but remained silent, waiting. McGee sighed. "Judge Alcott was a great man. A true man of dignity, integrity and honor. It broke his heart to find that he had sent an innocent man to prison for a crime his own son had committed. He put all his property here in Whitesboro in trust for the day you returned to the town. He took what remained of the funds he had and moved to Denver to live out the rest of his life. I've corresponded with him several times, and he's become a poor, weakened man, filled with remorse and shame."

McGee rose again and fidgeted with the things on his desk, picked up a few pieces of paper, laid them down, and crossed to the window. Jacob sat without moving, sensing that a howler of a storm was coming, a great conflagration that would change his life, something that he couldn't understand.

McGee turned, his large frame a dark statue in the glare of the hot afternoon sunshine behind him. He looked closely at the man sitting motionlessly in front of him and began to speak.

"Jake, don't say anything until I finish, please. It's possibly been as hard for me to meet with you today as it has been for you. When I first heard the accusations against you almost five years ago, I had no doubt of your guilt. As I took the depositions from the passengers and the stage driver, I believed every word they said and even more. I thought you a wild, reckless, uncontrollable boy. Unreliable, dishonest, wicked, lazy. I can see now that the boy I thought you were wasn't the boy who robbed stages, cheated at cards, or intimidated innocent victims for a foolish whim. The boy I've just described was Jon Alcott, not you.

"I believed every rumor, every lie, and every hint of trouble of which you were accused. On the other hand, I believed Jon to be trustworthy, hard-working and kind. As I look back now, I can see the difference. I can remember the honest way in which you played cards, never tried to win by tricks or slippery methods. On the other hand, I remember several times when Jon used those tricks to win and then laughed at the look on our faces when we lost. I now recall times I saw him in the shadows and alleys, hiding, I suppose, from someone who might suspect the real person behind the mask. I remember, especially, the earnest way in which you denied the accusations, and finally, the way you stood at attention, with your back straight and your head held high when Judge Alcott passed sentence; and the sweet and compassionate way you said good-bye to your father before the sheriff took you away from the courtroom.

"I've been prosecutor in many trials since I passed the bar, but that moment still haunts my sleep. And, the way Judge Alcott and his son spoke to each other during his confession. There was no affection, no honesty, nor strong feelings of bondage between the two men.

"It's taken me on a journey of self-discovery, just as it has been a torment to you, to know that Judge Alcott and I sent an innocent, though reckless boy to prison, when the real culprit continued to commit his crimes in silence. I don't suppose you can ever forgive us, but I promise you that I've learned to investigate further, to look at the facts more closely, and to judge more compassionately than I have before.

"As for Judge Alcott, he has no relatives. His only son is now dead. He's asked me to make out the papers to give you all his property in Whitesboro, so you can start fresh and clean among the people with whom you grew up. If you choose to sell everything and move away, everyone will understand. Take the money and start somewhere else, that's my advice. Buy yourself a ranch in Dakota, Montana or Texas, someplace where you won't be known to the town."

"What about my father's ranch? Is it mine?"

"Yes. Your father's will left it to you, and it's now in your name. He thought, despite your reputation, that you'd need a place to live and work until you decide what to do with your life. Of course, he never knew how the end would be; he thought you'd have to serve the whole ten years."

"So, if I want, I can sell Judge Alcott's possessions and live on my own ranch?" Jacob felt the river of his life about to change course. The anticipation blazed across him like the summer sun, roasting his thoughts into a white haze. His palms were sweating, and he sat in silent anticipation of the answer that would set his future in motion.

"Yes. If you want, I can sell the Alcott house and lots for you."

"Tell me the details. What do I own?" A smile crossed Jacob's lips, and he gazed at the lawyer with a touch of defiance. The smile changed to laughter as the details became clear to him, and for a time, he was once more the joyful boy who had once come to town with several dollars in his pocket after the sale of a few cattle or horses. When the discussion was finished, the two men shook hands, and Jacob walked from the office with a new purpose. His legs were no longer entangled with the leg irons of his past, and his feet seemed to float upon the soil. He crossed to the hotel and got a room for the night, went downstairs and bought a steak, with potatoes and gravy, and apple pie for dessert. He was so full that he felt he needed to walk off the heavy fare. He noticed but didn't react to the stares of the townspeople. He soared with the eagles, a rich man, and they no more than sparrows darting in fear. Among the raw-lumber buildings, along the main street with its board sidewalks, a few nodded (brave souls, or ones who were Johnny-come-latelies and didn't know him) and he nodded back but didn't speak. Others carried a look of fear and awkward silence, those who had sat in judgment of him. It was as well. They would learn him soon enough.

He wore no hat, as was common with the men he passed on the street, and not wishing to stand out more than necessary, he stopped at the general store, a balloon-frame building with thin walls and built of cheap deal board, to remedy the situation. The bell atop the door was the jangle of canyon wrens with their spilling of song, bright and joyous. Once the door returned to its frame, silence greeted him, that of dusk just before the frogs and night creatures begin their mating calls. Nothing had changed, and he smiled in the familiarity. It was as if time hadn't passed, and his years in the prison hadn't happened. There on the left were the canned goods and supplies for the farmers; on the right, shelves were filled with yards of cloth and sewing notions for the ladies; and in the corner where it had stood since the business had opened, sat the old pot-bellied stove, unlighted. Around it gathered several old-timers with a game of checkers, like pine cones fallen around the base of a tree, and near as prickly, too. Two ladies, wearing dresses that were architectural constructions of cloth and whalebone, whispered behind their fans. He waited patiently until they paid and were out of his way. He meandered to the back section where the clothing was kept, not wishing to hover unnecessarily. He could find his way around from remembered visits, and he spied the head coverings in several styles. Round-top silk bowlers, leather ones with wide bands for the sun, and a pink sort with feathers to appeal to the women. He tried on a couple of hats, found one to his liking and moved to the counter. A hush had fallen over the men who sat like the pine cones they resembled at the stove.

"Hello, Mr. Simmons." Jacob called the familiar name of the proprietor, a man he had known from his first memories. "I find myself in need of a hat. The sun gets mighty hot when you're chasing down cows through the gullies and over the hills. How much is this one?" Jacob smiled in a friendly fashion at the proprietor of the store.

"Two bits," came the quiet answer, though the man did little more than glance up and away again.

Jacob reached into his pocket and brought out a few coins, found a quarter and handed it to Simmons.

"Thank you, sir. Good day."

Jacob settled the hat firmly on his head and, with his stride as large as he could make it under the circumstance, left the store into a street that had begun to fill with layers of aromatic woodsmoke, telling of the dinner hour that would soon be upon them. Somewhere in the fog of cooking fires and belching chimneys, he was reminded of his time in the prison, and before he could correct his wayward limbs, his gait immediately returned to his shuffling, hesitant, previous method of moving.

He cursed himself under his breath for a fool.

— 3 —

Jacob rose early from his bed, determined to pull the load on yesterday. The memory of the passing events was as volatile as a flintlock pistol hiked up in his belt and ready to go off at any time. Bleary-eyed with lack of sleep, he stumbled to the barber shop for a shave and bath. He returned to his room with his dirty clothes in a bundle under his arm. No longer did he wear the suit from the prison; he had donned the new trousers, a blue plaid shirt, other necessary garments, as well as the new boots and his recently purchased hat. He felt more like the man he used to be. He ate a large breakfast in the hotel dining room and set off for the Methodist church cemetery.

The cemetery had been started only a few years ago, on land donated by a local merchant who needed a place to bury his infant daughter. It had grown to a considerable size considering the membership of the church congregation. He walked around until he came to the grave that he wanted to find. *Jonathan Petro Alcott.* The dates stood out boldly on the stone, and underneath was the notice, *A good boy turned bad.* Jacob read the words as though petrified at the inscription, the moon run in reverse, as the clouds of his thoughts obscured all else for a time. He swallowed the lump in his throat. He had expected some emotion, anger, bitterness, but all he felt was compassion for the lad. The numbers said that he had died at age twenty-six. That was the sad part, so young, at the prime of his life.

Jacob turned away and noticed the graves of Mrs. Alcott and the two daughters who had died in infancy. He felt in his pocket for the keys to the large house on the hill, which now belonged to him. There were five other keys. He owned the lots and buildings on which stood the leather goods shop of one Otto Frier, the dressmaker's shop of Miss Amy Roundtree, the home of Theodore Smith, but not his blacksmith shop, the Golden Eagle Hardware Emporium, the owner of which was Warren Goodwin, and the Truman Simmons General Store. In fact, counted all together, Jacob was a very rich man. He considered taking a look in the Alcott house but thought he would leave it to later.

He retraced his steps and stopped before the imposing door of the sheriff's office. It was his prison chains around his legs each time he faced it, but he would conquer the feeling. No reminder would again force him to shuffle his feet. It was his pride that counted, and he still had plenty of that. He entered and found a different deputy behind the desk, a man he had never met. He was told the sheriff was having his breakfast at the only decent restaurant in town besides the hotel, the Golden Lamb, so Jacob informed the deputy he would wait. He sat down in a ladderback chair on the front porch and leaned against the wall. He watched the pedestrians walking down the street and smiled at their reaction to his presence in front of the sheriff's office. The smile left his face when he saw Sheriff Whitaker Gomez coming toward him.

Jacob's memory took him back to the night the sheriff came to his father's ranch and arrested him for the crime of stage robbery. He could see once again the shock on his father's face and was certain the same surprise was reflected on his own countenance. He denied having anything to do with a robbery and carefully explained that he had been out with his father's cattle on the night of the attack on the stage. Sheriff Gomez, flashing well-shined leather and moving like a ghost soldier in the shadows, took him by the arm and shoved him toward the door. He yelled to his deputy, Max Gruggor, to saddle his horse, and they stood in the dark shadow of the house while the task was done. The long ride into town was taken without a word, and Jacob tried to imagine how such a thing could have happened to him. He prayed that the truth would be known as soon as the witnesses came forward.

The days turned into weeks, becoming a sepia-toned, dripping world, as the people of the town came by the barred window to stare. Then, the trial, the testimony of the witnesses, and the judge staring at him from on high with the look of the devil in his eyes. Jacob tried to hold his head high. He tried to stand firm and quiet when the audience burst out in a loud acceptance of the sentence. It sounded to him like the voice of doom. Ten years. Ten long, lonely years in the state penitentiary.

"Hale."

It was the deep, masculine voice that he had heard in the night so long ago, and Jacob was instantly on his feet, in the position of subservience that he had been cruelly taught by the warden and his guards with their night sticks and guns at their hips. But, he was a free man now. The sheriff's hold on him was only temporary. For two years, the warden had said, he must report twice monthly to the sheriff or another Law official in the Territory if the sheriff wasn't available.

Sheriff Gomez gestured that he was to precede him into the office, and Jacob meekly did as he was told. The lessons had been hard but clear. He walked through the door and stood quietly until the sheriff spoke first. The deputy quickly jumped from his seat behind the desk and looked at the man standing so stiffly in front of him. He didn't know the story behind Jacob, but with the harsh look on the sheriff's face, trouble was about to commence, and his hand stayed near his gun handle.

"Well, Hale, it's been a long time." The sheriff lifted a pen with a combined ink well and nib from the desk and held it between his fingers as he searched for the papers he needed. The hat on his head slipped to one side, and Jacob could see the bald spot on his head had grown larger. He found the papers he wanted and gestured for both young men to take a seat.

"Graham, you're new to town, so you haven't met Jacob Hale. Jake, this is my new deputy, Newton Graham."

The sheriff listened while Jake and Graham acknowledged the introduction, and he motioned again for them both to sit. The deputy took the chair at the back of the room, near the door, while Jacob sat near the desk. Jacob was surprised at the friendly tone in the official's voice. He had expected a more harsh treatment. He began to relax his muscles.

"Jake, I'm sorry I wasn't here when you arrived yesterday. Max told me you came by the office. I appreciate your attendance to the details of your provisional liberty. I didn't expect anything different when the warden telegraphed me. You were always an obedient youngster, in spite of your wild habits. Well, you've come to report in, so tell me. What are your immediate plans?"

"I don't have any, really, Sheriff Gomez. I talked to Alcott's lawyer, and he said I now own a considerable amount of property in the town, but I'm only interested in my father's ranch and the shape of the cattle and horses. Do you know the answers to that?"

"I was out there a few weeks ago. It seems to be in fine shape. Thomas Bladewell is still a top hand despite his age. And there's another hand you wouldn't know. Cliff Middenhaus, his name is. Comes from Montana, he claims. Nice fellow, a hard worker, but a drifter. I don't think he'll stay long now that you're back. Are you planning to work the ranch yourself?"

That wasn't a question Jacob had prepared himself to answer, and he looked at the sheriff blankly, unsure of his own intentions, and wondering what he would do next.

— 4 —

The ride from Whitesboro to his father's ranch was a lonely, solemn one, bringing to mind so many memories of the past to tempt him and so many years of anxiety, thinking he might not ever see his home again. Many nights he had awakened on his cot in the cell and tried to hide his emotions from his cellmate. There were several men who had occupied the same cell with him over the four-and-one-half years, but he never revealed himself to any of them, unwilling to pour his troubles into another man's safekeeping. He had bottled his dreams and ideas into a forbidden place within his mind, a deeply hollowed-out cavern as secure and private as a stone magazine for storing ammunition, and they remained there, safe and un-tried. He had no family left, and very few friends, if any of his old acquaintances still wanted to see him.

He was sure that Thomas Bladewell was such a friend.

Bladewell had been a callow youth when he wandered onto the Hale ranch, looking for work. An orphan, he had been drawn to the tough, war-hardened Zeke Hale and his gentle, lovely wife. What had kept him there was the bond between him and the soil. It went beyond the simple loyalty of a top cowhand to the brand for which he rode. He had fallen in love with the land, the gentle slope of the pastures near the house and barn, the far-off snow-capped mountains, the high, lofty trees on the ridge whose leaves turned scarlet and orange in the fall, and the craggy boundaries of the plains between the ranch and the town of Whitesboro. Even the cranky post oaks notched among the rocks, with twisted limbs that didn't have one straight section, were, to Bladewell, things to love.

It was this boulder-strewn boundary through which Jacob now rode. His eyes filled with tears as he crossed the line from his neighbor's property to his own. A few yards east ran the brook that fed the corn and grain fields his father had plowed and planted before Jacob was born. It was beside and in that cold stream that he had learned to catch fish and swim. There beside the shady brook he had taken his first sweetheart, Sue Blandon, on a lazy summer afternoon and asked her if he could steal a kiss. She said no, of course, and he had agreed to her wishes, but his dreams had been big and his ambition higher. He had thought he could wait until they were old enough and wise enough to marry.

Jacob stopped the unfamiliar horse and closed his eyes, tears running in a torrent down his cheeks. He'd thought of Sue Blandon Jordon many times in the past four years, of her grace and beauty, and her quick temper when aroused. When he received the letter from his father that she had married Tatum Jordon, his heart broke, and his emotions were so raw and real that he thought he would die from the pain. It was worse than being sentenced for a crime you didn't do. It was worse than the fear that you might be killed or assaulted during the night in prison. It was even worse than the pain when the message came from Sheriff Gomez that his father had died. It was a different kind of agony, a grief so intense that if he had had the free-dom to do it, he might have ended his own life. But, he had to keep going, to work hard, to hold his head high despite the slurs on his character and his name. His pride was now the only thing left to him. All else had been destroyed by a youth that he had thought was his friend.

Jacob clucked to the horse and gave him a gentle touch in the flanks, and he moved out from the spot of remem-brance. A thin, watery sun poured down with a shadowless glow as it slipped toward the horizon. He rode until he saw the light in the windows of the old house. It wasn't late, but the men must have had their supper by now. The barn nearby carved out a place for the animals at night or to park the wagons in bad weather. No life graced the black vol-umes of its doors. He rode slowly and took in the familiar vistas of his youth. The darkness was grown long and the shade trees heavy with leaves, but he could tell that Bladewell and Middenhaus had kept the place neat and tidy. The odd but familiar bur oak was silhouetted against the sky, more an anomaly in this windswept landscape than common. And while much was the same, he found small differences that let him know the years had passed here even as they had for him. He turned his head when he heard the familiar stamp of horses in the corral and the low of cattle in the distance. An owl hooted from a nearby tree, and he smiled at the sound.

"Hallo, the house. Anyone around to welcome a stranger home?" Jacob was taking a chance on the friendship of a lifetime, but he was confident that Tom would welcome him. There was the crash of a chair and a dish on the floor, and the door burst open with a bang.

"Jake? My God, is it really you? Why, I'd know you all to pieces from here to yon." Thomas Bladewell, now an old man, was down the stairs and had his arms wide before the younger man could climb from his horse. The familiar smell of tobacco and stale sweat and horse almost overwhelmed the boy as he was crushed until he thought his ribs would break. Another man stood silently by until the excitement slowly died down, then stepped forward to be introduced as Cliff Middenhaus. After removing the saddle and bridle and releasing Jacob's mount into the corral for the night, together the three men went into the house, where Bladewell stood unashamed with tears of joy in his eyes.

"Jake," Bladewell said, and his voice choked. The old man suddenly turned and left the house. Jacob understood. He looked closely at his hired hand, whom he had never seen before. He was a tall man, and much larger in bulk than either Jacob or Tom Bladewell. His skin was sallow and his eyes sunken in their sockets, and he was freckled like a guinea egg. He smiled, and the change surprised Jacob. His whole countenance was alive with mischief. He laughed.

"Never thought I'd see the day that old Tom Bladewell

turned soft and cuddly. You must be the young whipper-snapper who owns this broken-down old cattle ranch. To hear old Tom tell the tale, you must have come into the world already riding and roping the cows. Why, many is the time he's lulled me to sleep with tales of your expertise with the rope. And, here you are, in the flesh at last." Middenhaus took the ever-present toothpick from between his lips and spit into the fireplace.

"It's me, alright, but I'm afraid it'll take a while to get back into practice with the rope and branding iron. Took every inch of strength I had to keep sitting on that mangy saddle horse the livery loaned me. I guess you'll have to take him back tomorrow before he wears me down to the size of your toothpick. You may have to stop along the way and bell the animal, hobble it and set it to graze before you can go on. Not sure it can make the entire distance otherwise. Be prepared." Jacob said the words with humor, for he had decided he liked this man. His trust in him hadn't been in doubt, because Tom would never have hired someone he couldn't depend on, but he liked his sense of humor that could ease a tense situation.

"Okay, Boss. I'll see if I can handle him until he finds his own stall. If that's old Baldy you've been on, I can sympathize with you. Rode him myself a few times. Only thing that nag is good for is the glue factory. Got some hot coffee left in the pot if you're thirsty."

"Thanks. I could use a cup or two. I guess you know I've been incarcerated. I don't want anyone working for me who doesn't know where I've been holed up the last four plus years. If that bothers you, I mean, if you feel you can't trust me, I'll see that you have your pay tomorrow and something extra for your trouble." Jacob lowered himself onto the long bench at the table in the center of the room. His legs quivered from the time spent in the saddle.

"Sure. I allow to knowing all about you, Boss. The town's been buzzing for weeks about the way Judge Alcott and his son treated you. Tom's told me about the big frame-up. I never seen the judge, but if I had, I'd be mighty happy to give him a punch for old time's sake for you." He poured a cup of coffee for Jacob and sat down across the table with his own cup.

Jacob looked at his hired hand to see if he was backing and filling or serious. He seemed to mean it. He felt strangely pleased that a stranger felt so strongly about his mistreatment at the hands of Jon Alcott and his father. He was sad, too, for the judge was a good man. It was his son who had destroyed the good name he had earned in the Territory.

He took a sip of coffee and felt it flow down his throat and drop into his hollow stomach, like a black waterfall of steaming tar. It was a good feeling, too.

"You got anything fit to eat in this place? Anything will do. I'm so hungry, I could eat a bear, hide and all."

"Damn, I thought you ate in town." The hired hand rose so swiftly from the table he almost knocked over his chair. "Should have asked if you were hungry. It'll take a minute to heat over the beans and cabbage, and I'll fry up a rasher of some all-fired good bacon, if you like. I'm a fine cook. Even Tom says so."

"Anything. I'm bodaciously tired. I'll probably fall asleep before I get it half way down my throat." Jacob yawned, and he rubbed his face with his hands. "It's been a while since I've ridden a horse. Can't believe it took so much from me. Then, maybe it was the bigwigs in town that stole all my energy."

Middenhaus chuckled at the remarks, as he looked at his employer more closely. "Even in this dim light from this danged lamp, I can see a body at the end of his string. Your face is deathly pale, and it's no claptrap them hands are shaking. The glow I saw in them eyes a few minutes ago has ready faded to a dull shine. If this was a bucket shop, I'd pull out a dipper of gin for you this minute."

"It's not, I hope." Jacob smiled at the idea that Bladewell would allow a distillery on the property. "Just the rasher, that's all. I could eat it completely, I think. Haven't had a home-cooked meal in a coon's age."

Without another word Middenhaus turned to the sheet-iron cook stove fitted with pipes, adjusted the draft wheel and top lid, waggled the grate as he built up the fire, and warmed the beans and cabbage and fried several pieces of bacon.

Jacob closed his eyes. He knew the man was thinking he was weak. Truth to tell, he was. Weak and frightened of the future; tired and lonely and discouraged. He had seen the looks in the eyes of the townspeople. He had spoken with the deputies and suspected they would harass him about his past if they could. He had seen the fear on the face of Otto Frier as he quickly crossed the street. He had been on the jury that had convicted him. He would soon know that Jacob now owned his leather goods shop.

The food was set before him, and Jacob ate without speaking. He wished the man a quiet good night and crossed to his father's room. It was dark, and he stumbled a bit reaching for the lamp. He fumbled with the match safe, pulled out and ignited an old-fashioned white phosphorus friction match, set the wick alight and gazed around him in shame and regret. The smell of his father's aftershave lingered in the room even after two years. He could have recognized the scent in the desert awash with blooming cactus flowers.

Fully clothed, without a thought for the man in the kitchen, Jacob fell spread eagle across the bed, buried his head in his father's pillow and cried like a baby. He didn't hear the whispers of the two men in the house, nor did he feel the movement when his oldest friend placed a quilt around his shoulders and sat beside him in the only chair in the room. Bladewell laid a squareback Navy Colt five-shot revolver as big as a pork ham on the table at his side, turned down the lamp and guarded his friend until the dawn was slowly creeping over the distant hills, and the low clouds were painted in brilliant reds and oranges.

And, still, Jacob slept without moving.

*****

Bladewell rose, went into the kitchen and started a fire in the cook stove. From the flour keg, he dipped a portion of flour for the morning's biscuits. He poured coffee and water into the pot and placed it on the hot surface. He walked to the window and gazed at the familiar scene before him. He had left the house the previous night with the excuse of taking care of the stable horse, but he was so upset at the sight of his young friend that he was certain he would break down with pity for the lad. He tried to imagine what it was like to return to your home after four-and-one-half years in prison and couldn't. He tried to imagine what courage it must have taken for him to walk the streets of Whitesboro, with all eyes centered on his frame, watching, waiting for a mistake. Bladewell wasn't made of soft material, but he was softened by the sight of Jake in Ezekiel Hale's bed asleep. He resolved to protect his friend as he had protected his father in his final days. It would become his mission in life, until the man was able to take care of himself again.

— 5 —

Jacob didn't awaken from his restful sleep until almost noon. By that time, the bull's eye lantern in the barn had been lighted, the milk cow had been milked, the chickens fed and watered, the eggs gathered; and the hired hand in the person of Cliff Middenhaus was halfway back from town after delivering the borrowed horse to the livery stable. The town had now learned more of the situation surrounding the return of the Hale boy. Whispers had started long before dark, for women will talk, about his ownership of the big house on the hill and the five town lots.

A tangible fear now penetrated the thoughts of even those men and women who hadn't participated in the trial and conviction of the man. Rumors of revenge and tales of a wild boy turned angry grew into a torrent of guilt for those who had sat on the jury. Out of the twelve who had found him guilty, only five remained in the town. And, three out of the five lived in a house now owned by the same convicted man. What would he do? How would he behave? Those who had seen the shuffling gait, the trembling hands, now trembled themselves in anxiety and breathed with caution. They were the cause of his trouble, the town realized, while the guilty man, Jon Alcott, had gambled and drank and womanized, and they hadn't suspected the evil in his mind and heart.

Jacob, if he had known the extent of their anxiety, could have reassured them. For he had given instructions to the Alcott lawyer to set up a rent-to-own system where in a few months or years, depending on the value, the property would belong to the people who now resided there. He had no thoughts of revenge, only compassion for them. The lawyer, Frank McGee, could have quietened the rumors, but he received a certain amount of satisfaction in their plight, while fearing for his own safety, for he had been the prosecuting attorney. He knew the details of the transaction between Judge Alcott and the innocent man and anticipated a windfall if the situation changed in his favor. The sheriff and deputy, Maximillian Gruggor, watched and waited along with the townspeople, for they had had a part in the process, too, a large part.

*****

Jacob finished his breakfast and went with Bladewell in the wagon, a rough-riding, often repaired, but highly serviceable mode of transportation, for the thought of sitting astride a horse didn't appeal to him today. His shuffling stride was harder to control this morning, and his hands continued to tremble, while he cursed himself for being weak. They toured the area around the house and barn, and Bladewell explained how he had managed since Zeke Hale's death, without instructions from anyone. The sheriff came to visit occasionally to see that all was well, and the defense lawyer had come in the first year, but for the last fourteen months he had operated in the same way that he had learned from Jacob's father. Jacob looked without criticism or advice. He had plans and dreams, but he must first have a good idea of the situation.

The men returned to the house, and Bladewell left to complete his chores. Jacob positioned himself at his father's desk, and after a few minutes' reflection began to write on paper his plans for the near future. He heard the sound of a horse in the yard but didn't stop his pen nib from scratching across the rough paper until he looked up to see Middenhaus standing in front of him, a frown on his face.

"Come in. Come in. I don't bite, even if I am hungry." He hoped to get a smile from the cattle drover, but he was disappointed when he just stood quietly. Jacob lay down his pen and folded his hands.

"What is it? There's trouble brewing in town, isn't there?" As the questions poured forth, the drover relaxed and sat down in the stuffed chair near the fireplace.

"No, I wouldn't call it trouble. It's more like a rumble of distant thunder foretelling a storm coming in the night. The rumors are flying in town that you've returned for revenge on the men who harmed you. I didn't speak to anyone except the livery stable man, but I could tell from the nervous looks they sent my way, that they were wondering if I would take your side in the dispute. I hustled myself out of town as soon as possible."

"Why doesn't the sheriff speak up? Or, Alcott's lawyer? They both know that I don't plan to do anything except run this ranch."

"The sheriff knows that, and that shyster lawyer of Alcott's? I never did trust him." Middenhaus looked closely at Jacob with his eyes wide open, his expression revealing his sweeping and complete honesty. "But, I don't have any knowledge of anything shady he's been engaged in. I think you better tell Tom what's up and hear what he advises. He's a wise man. I'll go get him."

"No, he's busy." Jacob tapped the table for a moment while he gathered his thoughts. "It'll take a while until I have strength to work on my own. It's not that I'm weak, you understand, but it's this damned prison shuffle that I can't seem to get rid of. It's been years since I could stretch out my legs and go where I want."

"The best remedy for that is to take long walks and ride a horse. Toughen up your muscles." Middenhaus stood as if prepared to do his bit to help bring his boss' healing about.

"I know, and I will, soon. Sit down, Cliff. You don't mind me calling you Cliff, do you? The other handle is a mouthful." Jacob pulled the papers he had been working on closer to him. "I have here a few plans for the ranch. I won't explain the details until I have Tom in with us, but I want to build up the property, buy more cattle, a few horses, and a good bull. I'd appreciate any help you can give me in the way of quieting the rumors in town. Of course, they may not listen to you or Tom. It might be best if we just stay focused on the ranch and let the town take care of itself for a while. Do we have enough supplies for at least two weeks?"

"Possibly." Middenhaus looked thoughtful as he calculated the ranch's resources. "We can stretch the food supplies that far, if necessary. If we have to, we can always kill a cow. You own those, you know. But, coffee, flour, sugar, things like that, we have plenty if we watch what we do."

"Fine. Thank you for your warning and advice. Go on with what you usually do this time of day, and I'll explain tonight when Tom is here."

*****

If there were doubts in the mind of Cliff Middenhaus before, they were erased by his boss' forthright manner and honest acceptance of a man's opinions. Jacob Hale had won over the hired man to his side, whatever the outcome of his plans.

— 6 —

The smells of coffee and fried beefsteak permeated the kitchen of the Hale ranch as the three men ate heartily of the meal, cooked with somewhat clumsy action by the owner of the property. It had been a long while since Jacob had cooked a meal, but he hadn't forgotten the details. He could heave out a flour keg from the storeroom as well as anyone, and he knew the use of an ash hopper. He wanted the meal on the table when his hands appeared from their long day's work with the cattle and horses, for he had a lot to explain. He had spent most of the afternoon making plans and drawing maps. He hoped they approved of his plans, for he would need their help.

If the men were surprised at the offer of food, they didn't show it. Middenhaus had taken a chance during the afternoon as they had gathered wood, and tearing off a limb as big as a drainpipe, he had told Bladewell of his visit to town, and that Jacob wanted to discuss the future with them. Bladewell wasn't surprised but pleased that his young friend had taken the reins into his hands, for he had imagined last night that it would take longer for him to act. He reminded himself that it wasn't the man's mind that was weak, but his tortured body.

Middenhaus, as the junior member of the staff, rose from the bench with half a biscuit still in his mouth and began to clear the dishes, because he knew the boss would want the area empty to spread out his papers. He had seen the pile on the table in the living area.

Jacob, seeing his actions, rose and went into the front room. He grabbed the sheaf of papers, and picking up a pencil from his father's desk, paused at the entrance to the kitchen. His two hands were standing near and whispering to each other. A natural instinct for self-preservation caught him in the stomach, but he pushed it away. He had to trust someone, and if not Bladewell, who? He coughed and the men separated with a guilty look on each face. Middenhaus grabbed another handful of dishes, and Bladewell reached for the coffee pot and poured some into the cups.

Jacob walked as calmly as he could, attempting to lengthen his stride in a casual fashion, but it was useless. His legs wouldn't cooperate with his brain without a stilted, awkward, lurching step, and he resigned himself to shuffling toward the table, cursing under his breath. Tomorrow, he promised himself. While the men were working with the cattle, he'd walk a mile if it killed him. He had to get over this habit of thinking his legs were bound by chains.

When all three men were sitting at the table with their coffee cups in front of them, Jacob carefully explained his plans to his friends. First, he told them, he wanted to purchase about fifty head of cattle, more if Bladewell thought the land would support them. His father had run up to a thousand at one time. He knew nothing at the present time about the shape of the water resources or the grass, so he would need help with the matter.

Second, he wanted a new bull. Even if they had a dozen already on the place, the new cows would need to be bred to a good, strong bull with stamina. Bladewell would have to advise him on stock held by the neighbors, or whether they would have to go farther afield to find him.

When this news had soaked in, and the men had stopped exclaiming over the information, Jacob held up his hand for silence. He pulled the papers toward him and searched for a while until he found a hastily drawn, crude map.

"Tom, I know you've been here long enough to be familiar with the northern range, past the ridge with the heavy timber, and near the top of the divide."

Bladewell nodded his knowledge of the area, and Jacob looked down at the map and identified the area for Middenhaus.

"Five years ago, when I was searching for strays for Dad, I saw something I'd never noticed before. So, I did a little investigating. That's why I was so far from home when the stage near Garden City was robbed. At that season of the year, it wasn't expected that cattle would stray far from good grass, so no one believed I would travel such a great distance for no reason." He grinned, and this time he felt his excitement begin to build. "But, Tom, I saw what looked to be a natural split in the mountains. If a way could be built over the peaks and down to Whitesboro, it would save hours off travel from Denver. Instead of having to come by train from Junction, a person could drive a stage or a wagon. Eventually, a railroad spur might be built. I was so excited when I saw it, I could hardly wait to tell Dad. When I returned home, before I could speak, the sheriff stepped out of the shadows and I was caught. You know the rest; you were there. No one would listen to me. They didn't believe that I had been so far from our northern range without being up to some mischief." His voice had risen in excitement when he stated his news, but now it had dropped to a low murmur.

"I'd heard it remarked on," Bladewell mused quietly.

"Tom, while I was away, I spent as much time as I was allowed in the library, and I studied the process of building roads, engineering, it's called. If I can raise enough money with the cattle to hire a professional engineer and surveyor, I could show them what I saw and . . ." Jacob stopped speaking, and his eyes grew moist with excitement. It was the first animation for something substantial, something larger than him, that he had truly felt since he had returned to the ranch. Middenhaus looked at him in wonder, but Bladewell had seen him like this before, when he was a youngster at his mother's knees.

"Tell us, Jake."

"Tom, I have the money. Judge Alcott gave me all his property in Whitesboro. I own that monster of a house on the hill, and five town lots, as well. It's a miracle. I've been thinking it will take years to build that road, but it's possible now."

"So, Judge Alcott did you a favor, and in the process, did the whole town and maybe the Territory a favor, too." Middenhaus began to piece together the new knowledge he had received in the last twenty-four hours.

"But, Tom, Cliff, I can't use the money from the town lots because I promised them to the people who now occupy them. I told Alcott's lawyer to draw up the papers for a rent-to-buy proposition. As soon as they've built up enough equity, they can have a deed proper. I can't change my mind now."

Middenhaus thumped the table with a balled-up fist. "And as soon as news gets out that you plan to build a road through the mountains, that shyster lawyer will have a galvanized tin hissy and find a way of beating those people out of the property."

Jacob looked at Middenhaus as if he had grown horns on top of his head. "Do you really not trust McGee? Have you heard something we should know about him?"

"I'm sorry, Jake. The body's a fleshy shyster that needs to be exfluncticated. I don't have anything in particular against the man, it's just the way he moves around and his shifty eyes, like he's planning something evil." Middenhaus quelled his impulsive speech at the shadow that crossed Jacob's face.

"He was the prosecutor at my trial. He and Alcott were hand in glove for a great many years. Do you think, Tom, that he was in on the deal with Jon? Did he put out the rumors about me that I robbed that stage? I always wondered about that. Why did they pick me to accuse of the robbery? I'm not the only tall, thin boy with dark hair in the Territory."

There was silence for a long while in the old ranch kitchen, each man lost in his own thoughts. Middenhaus, having not been in the area at the time, didn't have the facts, but Bladewell knew. And he had been there in the courtroom when it happened.

"It's possible, Jake. Damn. I don't want to think on it, but it's possible he's been in from the beginning." Bladewell gazed at Jake with that compassionate look in his eyes. "Jake, this may be a trick. Judge Alcott may not have given you that property. Or, it may be a way to get his hands on the lots himself. It may be a way to stir up the townspeople against you. Tell us again, Cliff, what you heard at the livery stable this morning."

It was after midnight when the men finally concluded their conversation and went to bed. Overhead, the Dipper turned as if to pour out darkness upon the world. Jacob stayed awake long after the other men slept. He tried to remember odd events and things from the past, but at last, exhaustion overcame him, and he slept. He was resolved about one thing. He had to talk to Judge Alcott, to find out the truth about his property.

*****

As soon as the two working men had eaten and ridden out on their daily chores, Jacob Hale refilled the ink chamber in his father's pen, installed a new nib, and wrote a most polite and literate letter to the judge at his home in Denver. He pondered what he would say for a time, but in the end, he said what he intended, as though he had it in his mind all along.

The Hale Ranch,
Whitesboro
May 6, 1872

Honorable Judge Alcott
Denver

Sir,

Some years ago you presided over my trial, and that verdict is now overturned. The lawyer Frank McGee has told me of your generous offer to bequeath me property hereabouts. I wish to verify the details of the transfer of Real Estate and other Goods, as I have been away for some time. My man, Tom Bladewell, will bring up other matters with you, if you will allow.

I am most anxious to receive your reply. Please do not send a Telegraph. Tom is fully prepared to return your answer to me posthaste.

Jacob Hale

P.S. Sir, I am sorry for the loss of your son. I know it must have been a blow for the situation to turn out as it did.

He blotted it to ensure it was dry, folded it carefully and slipped it into a matching envelope. On the outside, he filled in the judge's name and address, care of the city of Denver. That chore complete, he set out to strengthen his body. He saddled a bay mare and rode around the ranch yard for an hour, and walked around the perimeter for another hour, carrying an old Model 1830 Springfield flintlock, hoping he didn't have to use it, as the muzzle flash was as long as a chimney brush. There was no news from town. No one rode or drove by the house.

*****

That night Jacob felt much more determined and discussed his plans with his hired men.

"See, Tom, you must find your way to the Denver stage, bypassing Whitesboro." Jacob took the letter to Judge Alcott out of a leather satchel and laid it on the table between them. Middenhaus sat to the side with his eyes taking in the scene. "This is to the judge. He'll know more about the truth of the situation. Perhaps McGee is being forthright with us, although we think not. The judge, if he chooses to help us, will be the one to verify yay or nay."

It was further decided that Bladewell would ride a horse to the town north of them to catch the stage to Denver, allowing him to circumvent the prying eyes of Whitesboro. He would carry the letter with him to ensure its safe delivery. It would take up to a week to go the long way to Denver. In the meantime, Jacob and Middenhaus would care for the cattle and other animals. Middenhaus would handle anything far from the house, while Jacob would remain near the house and do all the cooking and cleaning.

— 7 —

The plan worked to perfection. Before sunrise the next morning, Bladewell saddled his horse, one with good bones, a Copper Bottom breed whose Steel Dust lineage could be seen in its small ears, big jaw, and heavily muscled body, while Jacob cooked a breakfast of eggs and ham. The ranch hand was decked in riding boots with undershot heels, with the end of the spur straps shoved against the rowels to fix them and keep them from ringing. He wanted nothing that would clink as he rode out. Middenhaus saddled his horse with a Mother Hubbard saddle with a big, flat horn, full double rigging and a flank cinch to stabilize the saddle in preparation for riding the perimeter of the ranch to look for signs of trouble. He wore an 1840s infantry coat with a high band collar. All the insignia from that long-ago war was stripped away, and the fabric had faded to a uniform shabbiness. He would take a couple of sandwiches and an apple with him in case he didn't get back before dark. He assured Jacob that if he didn't return, not to worry. He took his pistol and his Henry rifle with him, making certain to carry a glove, since the Henry's barrel and magazine tube were too hot to be handled without one. He'd killed a right-smart of snakes and wolves with it, he allowed, and he was no fool when it came to handling a Henry.

Bladewell started out at the first sign of light, with a Colt carbine strapped to his saddle, and headed straight north, slogging through the wet grass. The handle of his Colt five-shot revolver protruded underneath his coat, making a bulge at his waist. From a certain point, he would head northeast. Both he and Jacob were familiar with the trail he would take. In case of trouble, Jacob could follow him, leaving Middenhaus to guard the ranch and animals.

The first day passed in a mixture of excitement and anxiety for Jacob. He rode a horse in the morning and again in the afternoon. He walked for an hour before lunch, again with the Springfield at his side, and once more in the afternoon, deliberately stretching his stride with each step. Middenhaus didn't return until long after dark.

"Any news, Cliff?" Jacob had the stove box heated and a meal in process as he'd promised. He refused to let the men down in his part.

"Just ordinary, as I'd expect on a regular day, Boss. I think we've managed to bypass the biddies in town who can't keep from telling every tale twice or more. We manage a few more days, and we'll be up the right creek sure enough."

Jacob had the food on the table by then, and Middenhaus ate a small supper and went to bed. The next day, he was up and riding in a different direction. He reported in each evening that all remained quiet.

On the fourth day, Jacob could walk without the shuffling pace of the prison chains. He rode farther and farther from the house along the road that was no more than two tracks with a strip of Indian grass in the middle to build up his strength but tried to stay within sight of the barn. As he had promised, he did all the cooking and kept the house clear of dirty dishes and clothes. On the sixth day, when he was beginning to worry about Bladewell, the man appeared on the horizon above the timberline. He gave a signal with his handkerchief, and Jacob rode to meet him.

They met under a stand of trees, dismounted, and after a short greeting of welcome, Bladewell handed Jacob a packet tied in brown paper.

"Been a good trip, no eyes to see what they shouldn't, and the judge was agreeable to hearing what you couldn't write in that missive. How've things been on the ranch?"

"Like a peach," Jacob allowed as he began to unwrap the packet.

"You've been working on that gait, I see. And you seem more comfortable astride than just a few days ago. I could tell both before you dismounted. I approve."

Jacob grinned at the compliment. Inside the packet was a letter from Judge Alcott, with the assurance that he had meant for him, Jacob Hale, to have the property in Whitesboro. He approved of the idea of passing the property to his tenants. He also sent along copies of the deeds of sale for each lot and a copy of his will. The last item was a copy of a personal letter to the town banker, Elias

Tammersham, to send him, Judge Alcott, at the earliest date possible, a copy of all transactions he had taken with regard to the property in Whitesboro since he had left the town and a record of any funds that had been withdrawn from his remaining account in the bank.

Judge Alcott said that he would search among his acquaintances for a surveyor, an engineer and a new lawyer-accountant who would handle his Whitesboro affairs in the future. Bladewell stayed long enough to rest and eat. Within hours of his arrival, he was on the road back to Denver on a fresh horse with supplies to last a week.

The calendar's pages rolled over, and it was five days later when he returned, riding on the train, with his horse in the baggage car. On the train sitting apart from Bladewell were three men in dark suits, with boiled collars, white shirts, and black ties. The first man to step from the train was Mitchell Prize, an experienced engineer, an expert in the building of road and bridges. The second, a short dumpy man with pink cheeks and a cheerful manner, was Frewin Fulton, surveyor for the territory and a friend of the governor. The third man to step down from the train was Gustaf Herndon, lawyer and accountant with the firm of Maxwell, Burns, Herndon, and Fitzhugh of Denver. Herndon, a large imposing man with red hair and an equally red beard, wearing a frock coat, knee-length, single-breasted, with a matching vest, followed Bladewell at a distance into the sheriff's office. The other two newcomers looked around for the hotel.

Thomas Bladewell and Gustaf Herndon talked for some time with Sheriff Gomez and left for the restaurant, where they enjoyed a hearty meal. The townspeople were used to strangers arriving on the train. However, an observant Amy Roundtree had seen the two men going separately to the sheriff's office, put the secret action in its proper perspective and confided in her friend Hazel Clark. She didn't see the other two men enter the hotel. That sighting was left to Mrs. Berta Simmons, wife of the proprietor of the general store. Between the two town gossips, the visit of the strangers was soon no secret. The question was, what did they have to do with Thomas Bladewell and Sheriff Gomez?

That burning puzzle was solved the next day, when a darker complexioned, no-longer-shuffling Jacob Hale rode into town on his favorite roan. He stopped at the sheriff's office, spent some time talking with Gomez, the two of them adjourned to the office of banker Elias Tammersham, and the three men tramped in a forceful manner to the office of Frank McGee, County Prosecutor. With a great deal of huffing and blowing from the accused, the sheriff marched McGee to the jail, where formal charges were taken out for embezzlement and fraud. The evidence for the charges of stage robbery or conspiracy to commit robbery couldn't be made until Judge Alcott arrived from Denver. He wouldn't be coming to preside over the case, but as a material witness against the accused.

As Jacob was arriving in the town of Whitesboro, Bladewell, Prize and Fulton were in preparation for leaving in a buggy borrowed from the livery stable and headed toward the Hale ranch. With all the excitement centered on the jail house door, no one spotted the three men traveling out of town on the road toward the ranch.

Leaving his roan tied to the hitch rail, Jacob left the

sheriff's office, drew a key from the pocket of his trousers and sauntered to the magnificent white house on the hill. Several women and a few men noticed with astonishment that he no long walked with a short, shuffling gait, as though he were chained, but climbed the hill with the stride of a determined man, bent on a mission. A few stared and dashed off to tell their most intimate friends. It was an exciting day in the life of the citizens of Whitesboro, but more was to come before nightfall.

He placed the key in the lock and entered the building in which no one had stood since the previous owner, Judge Alcott, had moved to Denver. Jacob made a quick tour of the rooms, both upstairs and down, came to a decision and exited with the same placid expression on his face. He went to the restaurant where he asked to speak with Mrs. Jackson Paul, widow and mother of two daughters. Mrs. Paul was very poor and had of necessity taken a position as cook and bottle washer. They spoke for some time, after which Mrs. Paul removed her apron and, collecting the key he placed in her hand, made her way up the hill, opened the door, entered and disappeared.

Jacob left the restaurant and went to the shabby house of Reginald Blair. Blair was known in public to be an expert in carpentry and plumbing fixtures. But, in recent weeks, he had been subject to spells of drinking whiskey when he could get it. After a few minutes of discussion Blair was walking behind Jacob up the hill to the Alcott mansion. He carried in his right hand, for he was left handed, the small wooden box holding his tools of trade. The two men stopped at one of the outer, boarded windows, discussed the problem at length, then the shorter, stout man used one of his tools to pull and yank off the board. With all the noise and motion, one would suppose that the man would break the fancy glass window, but he didn't. Satisfied that the man knew his job, Jacob turned from the house and went back down the hill. By this time, his legs were throbbing, and his head ached from the hot sun, but he wouldn't quit until he was finished.

The blacksmith shop being the closest to his house, he stopped there first. With a manner of charm and good will, Jacob convinced the man that he had no designs on his home. On the contrary, he discussed the terms in which it could be bought in a reasonable length of time. Leaving the smithy gasping for breath, he crossed over to Miss Amy Roundtree's millinery shop, finding her perched in the window where she could watch the outside activity without being seen. He ignored the woman's gasp of shock and proceeded to discuss, with a great deal of persuasion, that she would be able to buy her home, if she continued to make her usual monthly payments on time.

He proceeded to the hardware store and next visited Otto Frier's leather-goods shop and finally, his legs now aching in earnest, entered the Truman Simmons General Store, where he rested on a wooden box with Kilmeyer Beer, 50 bttls on the side, and not only won over the proprietor and his nosy wife with his good intentions toward them, but purchased a week's supply of groceries, for which he paid cash and promised to send his hired hand on the morrow to pick up. He apologized that he was unable to receive them now, but as they could see, he had come to town on a horse. A very surprised Berta Simmons ran to the home of Amy Roundtree, and by the time the sunset cast a lovely orange, pink and lavender hue over the town, the hostility that had advanced rapidly since his arrival vanished as quickly as it had begun. Within a month, every citizen of the town of Whitesboro was convinced that a great deal of harm had been done to a certain charming young man of their acquaintance.

Alas, the charming young man was no longer around for them to praise. He had left for the high mountains above the town with the surveyor and engineer. They pecked and pawed and surveyed, with Jacob holding the chain, and took measurements until the engineer's small copy book was almost filled with numbers and symbols and words. They moved their camp farther north and repeated the process. Two weeks later, the engineer and the surveyor took the train out of town, as they had arrived, with their tools, work books, maps and a great deal of money promised for the future road over the Continental Divide.

*****

On a rainy Friday in the month of September, a trial was begun in and for the County of Park, Territory of Colorado, with the honorable Judge William R. Belknap presiding. Frank McGee was the indicted party. The trial started in the usual manner, with introduction of the new County Prosecutor, Gustaf D. Herndon, duly appointed by the governor of the Territory, and the lawyer for the defense, one Warner S. Hardwicke of Garden City. The conviction was fully expected, as the proof gathered together was beyond reasonable question, and the trial wrapped up

131

in mere hours.

In the days following the trial, Judge Alcott shared that in his remorse over his son's failings, he had wished to see what Jacob Hale would do if he were given the property in Whitesboro.

"I had to know, you see." The judge and Jacob shared a meal in town at the Golden Lamb on the day before the elder man's return to Denver.

"Know what? I was in prison. I had no access to the property. It might have all gone to ruin." Jacob was humbled that someone would offer such a prize to a convicted criminal, not knowing if he would even want it.

"That was temporary, even if you served out your sentence. The important thing was to learn whether you would become a bitter, resentful, angry man, bent on revenge, and fall into the trap of lawlessness my son had. Or, would you use the property for the good of your neighbors and the future?"

The judge went on to give his deeper motivation. He had questions he wanted answered about the person he'd falsely imprisoned. What was the worth of the man? What lesson from his childhood would he carry with him into adulthood? Would he take the cruelty his son had forced upon him and turn it around for good?

Alcott admitted that he had seen something fine and pure and praiseworthy in the young Jacob Hale, even though his intellect had forced his hand to the stronger action of justice. It was the evidence at the time, he explained with great remorse, that swayed his thinking. He did what the evidence indicated, and decreed that Hale was guilty of the crime.

The real problem, he allowed, was that he couldn't see the evil in his own house. He opined that it was a moral stain that ran through humanity over and over, giving examples from the Bible where Samuel's sons were bad, good King Solomon was influenced in his old age by his many wives and their idol worship, and the kingdom that David had won, was lost.

Jacob reassured the elderly man. "I was brought up and nurtured by a war-hardened veteran, but I also had a lovely, gentle mother. I was taught the simple strength of honor and duty that sustained me through the bad times; I could no more seek revenge on my neighbors than I could treat my cattle and horses with cruelty." He considered his words to the judge, and he meant what he said. Revenge wasn't in his soul. Certainly, he could have burned down the big white house and destroyed the papers and books of Judge Alcott; he could have tossed the Simmons out on their ears, but it would be against his character.

Privately, Jacob knew the turning point in his life. Upon leaving his prison cell and venturing into the world, he'd wanted to rid himself of it all. None of it seemed important. All he knew was despair. When he came home and smelled his father's aftershave, the shame and regret he felt that his father didn't live to see him vindicated overwhelmed him. He rose from his bed determined that he would become the son of which his parents could have boasted.

*****

Over the years that followed, Jacob Hale prayed that

133

his actions would continue to make the world better for those who lived around him. Throughout his long life, he made it so, in the end willing the ranch to the State of Colorado for perpetual use as a state park for the benefit of anyone who might need to find rest and respite from their journey along life's road.

The Law and
Miss Eliza

— 1 —

The raiders hit the town of Crofton, Missouri, shortly after midnight on a cold, cloudy March night. Jumping off their mounts, a few of the men cleared the livery stable of its horses, using metal wedges to break the locks off the wooden doors, running through with oil lamps in their hands and opening the stalls. The horses whinnied and neighed, some more frightened than others, and a big paint by the name of Severance Boy kicked the wall of its stall, until it was bridled and given a bag of feed. Lifting leather bridles from pegs on the wall, the rest of the animals were readied and led snorting and prancing into the night.

More men broke the lock on the general store for supplies, weapons and bullets. They were less careful than those in the livery. Shelves were tumbled over, a bag of flour was sliced open and strewn about and glass jars were broken just to hear them shatter. Several women's premade dresses were bandied about with crude laughter, but they broke open weapons cabinets and emptied drawers of ammunition as they joked, until the pouches they carried over their shoulders bulged and strained to close.

One pair roped the church bell, sending it clanging into the night. That woke the town, but it was the gunshots fired into the prized stained-glass window that let the people know what was happening. One of the ruffians caught sight of Opal Mae Kellogg, a saloon girl, just leaving her place of business, and he grabbed her and gave her a fierce kiss. Just before they rode into the night, they pulled their horses up at the bank. They tied ropes around the sign and pulled it down, before removing a cut log from one man's saddle and shattering the plate glass window. They set two sticks of dynamite at the safe door, and with an explosion that shook the building, smoke and dust came pouring out. They absconded with as much as two saddlebags would carry before mounting their beasts and shooting their guns in the air; and whooping and laughing, they rode out of sight.

It happened so quickly that only the sheriff, Micah Robertson, and his night deputy got in a few shots at the bandits before they made their way out of town, pushing the newly captured horses ahead of them. Men began running out of their homes, with the school teacher, Tobias Moore, still fighting to get his pants on, with a gun in one hand. He fired it off, only to have it hit the porch railing, shattering the wood and creating a small panic. Sara Lancaster, from the milliner's shop next door, had just stepped outside to see what was happening, and she swooned to the floorboards, with her hand dramatically at her forehead.

Four men, including Joshua Hammer and Mort Finne-gan, the town barber, managed to round up several horses, and saddled, they mounted the beasts to form a posse to head in pursuit.

On their way south, the raiders stopped at the Jennings' farm. No one was later able to say why they picked that particular one, when there were several other farms closer to the town. It wouldn't have been a first choice for prime pickings, as the farmer was a widower with three young girls, and the once-prosperous farm was isolated, with the family cut off from interaction with the townsfolk by the townspeople's cruel and callus actions and by Thurston Jennings' crushing grief and love of drink.

Hearing the rumble of running horses on the road to town, Jennings made a fatal mistake. He stopped long enough to put on his britches. By the time he grabbed his shotgun from above the mantle, the majority of the raiders not engaged in the herding of the newly acquired horses from the town had stolen his two horses, the milk cow and the chickens, and set fire to the barn.

"Hey, you sods!" He cursed as he stumbled across the floor, his head still reeling from the previous night's bout of drink. "This is my farm. Get yourself off my land."

The man took no regard for waking his sleeping daughters, nor the fact he couldn't be heard by the marauding invaders. The glow of the fire lit up the night, and he hit the door at a run, his pants still not buttoned, and sent a shot into the night air. One of the raiders aimed his pistol directly at Thurston's chest and fired the fatal shot.

Now, angry that their raid had been witnessed, half a dozen of the men climbed down from their mounts, and shoving the still-breathing Thurston Jennings aside, scrambled into the house.

"Hey, in here! We've hit the motherlode. We'll eat for a week." One of the men had found the kitchen larder, grabbed a canvas sack and started throwing a cooked ham, potatoes and ears of corn into the bag.

"Biscuits!" One of the men, with dirty blond hair and a filthy shirt, dropped his rifle carelessly on the kitchen table and scooped up several, shoving one in his mouth and the others in various pockets. "Eat 'em quick before Ox gets in here." The first man laughed as he thrust washed carrots in with the ham and potatoes. Half a freshly baked pie was uncovered under a dish towel, and the men, laughing, stuffed handfuls of pie in their mouths.

The largest and meanest of the group found thirteen-year-old Eliza Jennings in her bed, startled awake by the noise and confusion of the gunshots in the night. He was a huge man, with dark hair and an angry scowl on his face. He pulled Eliza from her warm bed, threw her on the floor, and took her innocence from her. He laughed and asked if the others wanted to participate in the fun. Eliza was never sure how many men used her that night. She thought four, but she mercifully fainted before the ordeal was finished.

By the time the sheriff had formed a posse to follow the tracks of the horsemen south, the raiders and their stolen bounty had split into three groups and disappeared into the forest. Sheriff Robertson, not yet thirty and unmarried, stopped long enough to divide his men into three groups to follow the tracks, but two of the groups gave up when the sign was lost among the dead leaves and humus of the forest floor. The wind began to blow more fiercely, and a slow, icy rain fell on the men as they turned back to their wives and a hot breakfast.

The stragglers of the posse coming back toward town late in the afternoon smelled the smoke from the smoldering fragments of the Jennings' barn and found the farmer's body still lying near the front door of his log cabin, his useless shotgun clutched in his hand. The rain was now coming down at a steady pace. Puddles of water and ice covered the ground near the hapless farmer's remains. The blackened ruins of the barn cast a heavy gloom over the site of the tragedy. Sheriff Robertson looked up and saw a couple of buzzards catching the air currents and waiting their turn to pounce on the body.

"Look sharp for evidence to convict the raiders," Sheriff Robertson yelled to his men, as he moved through the house and heard crying children. He found Eliza Jennings on the floor of her bedroom lying only partially clothed in a pool of blood, barely breathing, with her nightgown crumpled around her waist. With his eyes averted, he gently tugged her clothing to cover her person. Her two hysterical sisters were hiding in a cramped space behind a draped quilt among the family's clothing and shoes. One of the sisters, Clothilda, held her pet dog in her arms, trying to draw comfort from the warmth and substance of the animal, but the dog was whining and shaking as much as the frightened children.

"Jim, we need some warmth in here. Can you see about a fire in the stove? Maybe some hot coffee before long, if Jennings had any around." The sheriff instructed his permanent deputy, Jim Potter, to light the kitchen stove and get some warmth into the house. The deputy grumbled his acceptance and headed to the wood pile just outside the back door, for there were only a few sticks and old newspapers in the metal holder behind the stove.

"You, Sullie, how about drawing up some water? Jim's getting the fire, and we need some of that water heating on the stove." Water, lots of water, the sheriff directed, pulling several metal buckets from a corner, when Sullie seemed confused at just what the sheriff meant.

The men, about a dozen in number, all gathered around, hoping to see what had excited the sheriff so much. Most of them drew a gasp of surprise at the sight of the injured Jennings girl lying in her own blood.

"Micah, they done killed her," the town barber, Mort Finnegan, moaned.

"Perhaps soon enough, but we've got the two sisters to think of. We need this cleaned up, so they don't have to see it. The porch outside, also." The sheriff rested his eyes on the immobile, bloody form for a moment and shook his head.

Several of the men started from the room in shock and nausea, barely finding the front porch before losing their stomachs, and in the process, disturbing the two younger girls. But, the sheriff calmed the sisters and told them to stay close by, instructing Finnegan and the town doctor, Rory Putnam, to take care of them. He gently gathered the older girl into his strong arms and laid her on her bed, covering her with a couple of quilts. He didn't try to examine her for wounds or awaken her, thinking she would soon follow her father to the nether world. He was more concerned with the little ones.

The dog, Rastus, at last free from the bondage of his

young friend's arms, ran from the room and out the door. He stopped for just a moment at the sight of his master's body, sniffed and poked at it, but suddenly hustled into the grass to relieve himself after the long day's travail. One of the men tried to catch him when he returned, but he ran into the icy rain toward the ruins of the barn, where he stood whining and sniffing the ground. He set up a loud howl of misery that all the sheriff's men thought would follow them for the rest of their lives.

Once Potter, the deputy, got the stove to going, he poured water from the small pump at the kitchen sink into a kettle and a large pot and set them on the stove to boil. Sullie Jackson, the night deputy, had made his way to the larger outside pump, and while the rain had darkened his shoulders and hair, several buckets of water now lined the back stoop, ready for whatever Potter and the sheriff needed. The sheriff went into the room to see how Potter was coping with the water and told him he didn't think the girl would live, but they'd best send to town for one of the women to come help her. Potter turned his duties over to Jackson, moved into the group of men in the parlor, huddled, smoking and gossiping over what they had discovered this day, and got their attention.

"Anyone wanting to ride back to town with me, come along. Micah's staying with the victims of the raid."

"The eldest girl, is she gone?" That seemed to be the general question, and Potter shrugged.

"Haven't checked. Micah thinks before long. I'm out to my horse. Follow if you will."

Most of the men, although it was miserable riding in the rain on horseback, went to town with the deputy, hoping to be the first to spread the news of what they had seen.

Two men stayed behind. One, a saloon keeper and gambler, James McBeth, had witnessed the death of his own wife and children in North Carolina at the hands of hostile Indians, and he felt compassion toward the young girl.

"Aye, Sheriff, you know nothing good's coming from this. I'd like to stay to help, if you'll let me."

"You know you're welcome, and I could use you to spell me from time to time. I feel the need to keep a lookout for the night. Who can tell if the raiders will return."

The other man, Paris Hamilton, a grizzled old timer who had taken to drinking when told he was too old to join the Union Army and save the nation from just such wasteful destruction, began to talk of politics and the cruelty of war, but the sheriff stopped him before he got into his usual rambling speech, for the sheriff had his own memories with the army from a previous war and had never forgotten the experience. He didn't need to hear Hamilton's fancies during this desperate time.

"Men," the sheriff told them, when everyone else was gone, "you can best help by shifting Jennings' body onto his bed and feeding the survivors. The two smaller girls will need breakfast, even if their father's dead. You can get Sullie to help."

Now that they had something helpful to do, the two men were quick to obey the sheriff. They first grabbed an old blanket from the sofa in the parlor, then covered and lifted the heavy body of Thurston Jennings and laid him on his bed to await the care of the women. Neither had known the man well, he being a lone farmer a few miles from the town, and they being city folks, but they used as much care as possible in handling the body. The rain had washed away all signs of the killing from the front door of the house, for which Hamilton at least was thankful, for he was certain that once the women from town arrived, they shouldn't be greeted by the gristly sight of death. He suggested that he and McBeth use some of the boiling water to scrub the floor where the young girl had lain.

Working as a team, they talked softly to the girls while cleaning the cabin and started a meal from the remains of the larder, while Jackson rounded up eggs from several chicken roosts among the trees. Hamilton was especially good at making biscuits, he said to the girls. He finally enticed the eldest of the two, Margaret, to help him find the flour and lard and proceeded to mix the batter. McBeth claimed Clothilde's attention by taking a book from the shelf beside the fireplace and sitting down to read aloud. Soon, the young girl became enthralled by his calm, quiet monotone and was fast asleep in his arms.

Meanwhile, the sheriff moved to the ruins of the barn, hoping that some sign was left of the bandits and murderers. But, all he found was the miserable dog howling at the smell of destruction. He tried to catch the animal, but he backed away and went back to the spot in which he had first attached himself. The sheriff thought maybe there was something there, so he shooed the grief-stricken dog away. He found a stick and started sifting through the blackened ruins. There, covered by the half-burnt wood, Robertson found a man's leather glove. He picked it up carefully by the edge, and the dog went berserk. Jumping and barking, he sniffed the glove and then ran toward the woods. When the sheriff didn't quickly follow, he came back, grabbed at the sheriff's britches leg, and yanked. Then, withdrawing his teeth, he headed again toward the forest. The sheriff was certain the dog smelled the scent of the raiders. But, it was getting late in the day, and he was responsible for the welfare of the three young survivors until the women from town arrived. Disappointed, for he was sure that was where his first duty lay, he gave up the opportunity to follow the trail and went to the house. The dog headed down the path the raiders had taken and never returned.

Inside the house everything was calm and peaceful. Sheriff Robertson was surprised at the sureness with which the two oddly matched men had gained the attention of the girls. One girl was talking to old Hamilton, while he sliced thick pieces of ham from the bone. The other was asleep in the arms of a saloon keeper and gambler, whom the sheriff had often thought dishonest in his poker games. Passing them by with a nod of the head, he found a news-paper in the wood box and wrapped the glove in it. He nod-ded at Jackson sitting at the kitchen table and made his way back to the parlor. McBeth started to say something, but the sheriff looked at the sleeping girl beside him and shook his head. Later he would tell them the details.

Laying the dog's newspaper-wrapped gift on the fire-place mantle, Robertson walked into the bedroom to check on the girl. She was awake and lying in the bed with her eyes open, but when she saw him enter, she started scream-ing. He pointed to his badge and told her to be calm, he was Sheriff Robertson, and her sister was asleep in the other room with his deputies. She calmed down and edged to the far part of the wide bed, away from him, with her eyes reddened in the paleness of her skin. He could see the fear in her manner.

"Now, don't fret yourself, young lady. Some women are on the way from town to help you and your sisters. The cursed men have gotten away into the forest, but with God's help, we'll find them, or the Union Army will soon know of what they did to the town and your father. I'm sorry, but your father is dead. We've laid him in his bed, if you'd like to see him later, after the women have come. One of my deputies is cooking some ham and biscuits, with some eggs we found in the roosts, so your sisters will be taken care of soon. Is there anything you want to say about what happened to you and your father that might help me in my investigation?"

The sheriff looked closely at the girl, trying to see if there was panic in her face. But, she seemed calm enough after his explanation.

"No. Thank you kindly, sir. What's done is done. Are my sisters well?"

"The girls are fine." The sheriff read the meaning behind her words; she was asking if her sisters had been also accosted. "We found them hiding in the closet, or what looks to be a closet, among the clothes and shoes. They had the dog with them, too, keeping him quiet. Mayhap the men didn't even look for them there."

"Oh, thank God. I was so afraid they'd been hurt." Then, with tears forming on her cheeks, she covered her face with her hands and wept. Sheriff Robertson turned his head aside, trying not to startle her with his embarrassment. They both heard wagons and horses in the barnyard at the same time. She withdrew her hands and looked at the sheriff with a question in her red, tear-stained eyes.

"That'll be the town folks. You wait here. I'll send the ladies in to help you clean up and dress." He walked out, closing the door gently behind him.

Just as the handle clicked, he heard her call out, "Sheriff Robertson!" He turned, opened the door and put his head back in the doorway.

"I must write to my uncle in Clay County to tell him of his brother's death. He'll come to us, I'm sure. Would you find some paper in my mother's secretary and a pencil, please? And, tell my sisters I'll soon be out to comfort them."

The sheriff paused. He was almost twenty-seven years of age and had seen a lot of tragedy in his time as a peace officer, but he couldn't recall a single time when a young girl, who couldn't be above twelve or thirteen, had remained so calm after an experience such as this. Her only concern was for her sisters' fate, not her own. She must have witnessed the death of her father, for she hadn't acted surprised when told of it. Maybe later, when the shock wore off, she could recall more details for him, but for now, he must deal with the aftermath.

The front room was filled with people. There were five women, genteel ladies of some distinction from the town, all clucking like hens in a barnyard. The men were in various poses, some talking with the ladies, and some in the kitchen with Hamilton, who was seated near the girls. The two girls, seated on a bench at the table, were trying to eat, their faces streaked and red from crying.

Jackson, the deputy, trying unsuccessfully to restore

order, held up his hand. "Ladies, gentlemen, please have some respect for the grieving daughters. Quiet, please." He paused a moment, and peace was restored. "Mrs. Carson, Mrs. Stimson, if you please, the girl in yonder room needs your attention. Take some warm water and towels with you."

Bertha Carson stared at the deputy, and then as though realizing there was another sibling in the home, quickly grabbed a cloth and took the kettle of boiling water from the stove. She moved toward the back room. Mary Louise Stimson, called to her duty as a Christian woman, took off her hat, gloves and cape, piled a plate with food cooked by the hands of Hamilton, and followed Bertha.

Martha Randle seemed to come out of the trance into which she'd fallen at the sight of the two weeping girls and walked over to them. She was a buxom, jolly lady and soon had the girls laughing and eating their meal. Within minutes, the other two ladies had cleaned the house and the dishes. They didn't comment on a few drops of blood at the front stoop that McBeth and Hamilton had missed in their hurried cleaning chore. One of the women dashed some water on the drops, while the other one scrubbed with the broom.

Hamilton told the ladies where he'd found the kitchen supplies, then, relieved of his duty, walked outside, taking the rest of the men with him. The rain had stopped falling, and the men gathered near the remains of the barn, discussing what was to be done about the situation.

Sheriff Robertson relaxed at the sound and sight of such activity. He moved to the table in front of the window, but it held no paper, only a lamp and a Bible. Then he saw what must be a woman's small writing desk and opened a drawer. No paper was in it, only some thin handkerchiefs and children's toys. He opened and closed another one. It contained a pile of scattered letters and a bundle of unused envelopes. Inside a third drawer, he found a few sheets left in a child's tablet and a pencil, ground down to a nub with the many sharpenings it had undergone, an assortment of quill pens and a bottle of India ink. He took the objects to the door of the bedroom. Calling out to the ladies inside, he handed in the objects, telling Bertha Carson, who answered the door, what they were for. He planned to personally see that the letter caught the early morning stage on its way east.

He walked outside and joined the congregation of men at the barn. It was a sad sight, and the smell of burnt wood and manure-soaked straw hung in the air like a blanket. The men shifted through the rubble and found a few pails and metal boxes that could be salvaged. A rake with a charred handle, a leather saddle that might survive the damage of smoke and fire, a barrel of nails and a child's wagon were all that could be dragged from the wreckage. The sheriff opened one of the small metal boxes out of curiosity and found a handful of gold coins. He quickly closed it and hid the box from the sight of the other men. He would come back for it later and see that the girls benefited from the contents.

Within an hour most of the men and women had gone, leaving only the sheriff, Bertha Carson and Mary Louise Stimson behind. As the men left, the sheriff told them to get a good night's sleep, for Deputy Potter planned to take the glove and leave with them early in the morning to see if they could pick up the dog's trail. Maybe the animal would lead them to the raiders.

After the daughters of Thurston Jennings were asleep in their beds, the two women prepared the body for burial. Hamilton, McBeth and a few other men had promised to come early in the morning when the ground was drier to dig the grave. They would bring their own tools and begin the heavy duty of destroying the remains of the barn and clearing the ground. It was a matter of large speculation whether another barn should be built on the site, or whether the girls should be taken into the hands of the town council and adopted out to the local citizens. In that case, the land would be sold at auction. The sheriff told them that the girls had relatives in St. Louis, but the townspeople ignored his information.

The sheriff took his rifle and looked for footprints, or other signs that might help Potter trace the raiders' direction from the farm, but everything was obliterated by the rain, mud and the recent tracks of the townspeople's horses and wagons. He took a blanket from the house and walked to a slight rise of land, prepared to spend the night as guard over the place. It was a cold, calm night with a million stars in the sky. Sometime around midnight, a small crescent moon appeared and gave a glow to the tin roof on the house. Inside, a lamp was left burning on the table near the window of the front room, and occasionally Robertson could see one of the ladies walk past, keeping their own watch over the girls. Early in the morning, when he was half asleep, he saw a stealthy, feminine figure emerge from the house. He watched closely as the woman walked toward him. He called out to give her his position.

Bertha Carson saw the sheriff stand up and signal his location, and she moved toward him. The night air was brisk and held a dampness left from the earlier rainfall. She shivered as she came up to Sheriff Robertson.

"I was restless," she told him. "I don't mind staying in the house with the girls and the dead body, but I couldn't stay a moment longer listening to the monotonous tone of Mary Louise Stimson as she regaled me about her rheumatism and her dreadful headaches. When the woman finally wound down and appeared to drift off to sleep, I put a few pieces of wood in the stove and heated the coffee. If you like, I could cook up a few rashers of bacon and scramble a quartet of eggs for you and me." She wore her warm woolen scarf and coat. A widow some half-dozen years older than the sheriff, she had opined to others in town that he was an attractive man, still in his prime of life.

"Now, Bertha, why would you want to do that? You'd wake the entire house."

"Micah, I thought you must be hungry, sitting out in the cold like this." She took the cloth from the box in which she'd put two cups of coffee. Steam rose from the cup as she handed one to the sheriff.

"Why, thank you, Bertha. That was very kind and thoughtful of you. But, you should be asleep like the others. Dawn will be here soon and the men from town arriving to begin the burying."

Sheriff Robertson knew well the schemes of widows and single women. He'd been avoiding entanglements with women like Bertha Carson for over five years. He took a few sips of the coffee while standing at attention. He didn't speak as he watched her for signs of flirtation.

She tried to huddle closer to him, but he moved away, for it would give her a notion of friendliness he didn't feel. As soon as he finished drinking, he handed her the cup and ordered her back to the house.

"Let the girls sleep as long as possible. It'll be a sad morning for them. I'll be in to check on them when the sun comes up. Try to get some sleep yourself." He watched as Bertha returned the empty cups to the box and marched back to the house, a frustrated and angry woman. He was certain he'd made an enemy, but he wouldn't be trapped by a woman into some compromising position. His job as sheriff depended on a certain aloofness from the citizens of the town. He wanted no gossip to hang over him.

— 2 —

After sleeping through the afternoon and night, Eliza was awake before the dawn. She'd eaten a small piece of ham and a hunk of bread before falling asleep, so she wasn't hungry. She needed to go outside, though. She slipped from her bed, and trying not to call attention to herself, she crept past the two sleeping women in the parlor and let herself out the door. It was a beautiful night. She looked up at the stars and wondered how the world couldn't have changed in some way. She was changed. Her sisters would be changed. She wasn't sure they could ever trust a man's actions again. She observed the shape of a person on the ridge above the blackened area where the barn had stood. She supposed it was the sheriff or his deputy but didn't concern herself with the matter.

She let herself back into the house and drew a glass of water from the pump, hoping the sound didn't awaken the ladies. She took it with her and returned to her room. It wasn't the pain of her bruises, nor the thought of her lost virtue that kept her restless. It was the sound of the gun shots and the fall of her father's heavy body onto the ground that kept repeating in her mind. He'd called out to her in his last minutes. But, she couldn't help him. That was her greatest regret. Her father needed her, but she couldn't move from her place on the floor. Her mind tried to reject the actions that followed her father's fall, but they demanded to be brought forward.

She took a sip of the water and sat on the edge of the bed. Why? She wanted to know why the raiders had stopped at her home. Taking another sip from the glass, she let the horrible thoughts have free rein. She saw again the craggy, pockmarked face of the large man, as it came closer to her. She felt again the sting of tears in her eyes, as he kissed her with wet, slimy lips. When he finished, he boasted to his friends to come take their turns, and they did.

It was the thought of the fourth man, the one the others called Ox, that made her want to take a gun and seek vengeance. She felt shame and anger as she recalled his treatment of her. Large and unkempt, almost as massive as the first man, Ox had removed his belt and whipped her several times on the back, and then used it to tie her wrists to the bedpost so she couldn't escape. Her last thought of him was his hard bite on her ear and the warmth of blood as it soaked her neck; and his screeching voice as he yanked her hair as though it were the reins of a horse. Eliza forced herself to recall the details of the ordeal, so she would never forget.

She sat on her bed and swallowed the last of the water in her glass, then crossed to the table, where she found the remains of the child's tablet and pencil. She began to write down everything she remembered, the color of their hair, their eyes, even though it had been dark, so she could describe the men. Not just for evidence for the sheriff to punish them, but also as a source of comfort for her. Maybe writing the details would bring some peace to her mind. The sky was beginning to turn pink on the eastern horizon when she finished. She used every inch of the paper, even writing along the edges when she ran out of pages. She folded it neatly, placed it under her pillow, blew out the lamp, and fell into a deep, refreshing sleep.

*****

Mary Louise Stimson, lying on the sofa in the parlor pretending to be asleep, heard Eliza get up and listened closely, but couldn't hear the sound of the scratching pencil on paper. She heard an occasional moan or cough and waited to be called for help, but no such plea came. She looked at Bertha Carson, snoring softly in the one good horsehair chair, and wondered if Bertha really cared for the girls' well-being or was trying to impress the sheriff. Married herself, Mary Louise had little compassion for the widows seeking another husband for the status it would provide. It was sad to be alone, she knew, but to throw yourself at a man was beneath contempt. She moved cautiously, for her rheumatism hurt especially bad in the dampness of the night air. She saw the light go out in the bedroom and slowly fell into a deep sleep.

At dawn, Mary Louise rose refreshed from her nap on the sofa, picked out some large kindling from the box and started the fire in the kitchen stove. She yawned as she adjusted the damper. She made coffee, for she knew that was the first thing the sheriff would look for when he came in after his long night in the darkness. She found the flour and lard and began to make biscuits. She was rolling the dough onto the table when the sheriff walked in, stomping his feet on the floor to shake the mud from his boots.

"Ah, Mary Louise, I could smell the coffee, and it drew me inside. 'Tis a dreary morning to be sure. But, soon the sun will be up, and it'll quickly chase away the chill." He poured himself a cup of the brown drink and sat at the kitchen table, silently watching the woman working at the stove. The warmth from the fire left his eyes half closed, for he had been up all night.

*****

The sound of stomping feet and a male voice awakened Bertha Carson from her slumber. She was puzzled at first until she got her bearings, then quickly rose to her full height of five feet. She was embarrassed at being caught asleep by the sheriff, but the man ignored her rustling sounds. She reached her hands to her hair to bring it into some kind of order, then walked to the outhouse. When she returned she bustled about the kitchen, helping Mary Louise with the breakfast. The sheriff was seated at the kitchen table, slowly sipping his coffee.

A sound came from the back of the house, and in minutes, two small girls came clambering through to the kitchen, laughing, and stopped dead at the sight of strangers in the room.

"Papa? Liza? Where's my papa?" the larger girl asked with tears in her blue eyes. Quickly, Mary Louise stopped her chores and drew the girls into her arms.

"Good morning, girls. I think you must be hungry. My name is Mrs. Stimson, and this is Mrs. Carson and Sheriff Robertson. Don't you remember us from last night? We've been here since yesterday morning." She drew the girls over to the bench and seated them. She worked the pump and soon had two glasses of water in front of them, chattering all the time about the sunshine falling on the floor and the birds singing outside the open window.

*****

The sound of the girls' laughter awoke Eliza, and she quickly dashed some icy water from the pitcher onto her face, dressed in a clean frock and went into the kitchen. She felt sluggish and tired, but the thought of her sisters moved her to action. She placed the tablet with her remembrances beside the sheriff's place and went to hug her sisters. She had a smile on her face, as though it were an ordinary day. On the peripheral of her vision, she saw the sheriff thumb through the pages of the tablet, nod his head toward her and continue sipping his coffee. She greeted the two women and poured herself a cup of the hot, weak coffee. She didn't criticize the taste. She began to praise the two women and ask if she might help them in some way. She was told to sit and eat her breakfast, as they had everything in hand.

Indeed, they did. The two women bustled about the kitchen as though it were their own home. When the girls had finished, Eliza took them to their room, brushed their hair and helped them don fresh, clean clothing. She assisted them in tying their shoes. She couldn't help hearing the conversation going on in the kitchen as she was reminded of the seriousness of the day. At last, there was no excuse for hiding, so she joined the adults in time to help with the cleaning up. She seated the girls at the table with a picture book for each of them and told them to read aloud the words. She looked for the sheriff, but he had eaten and left the room.

In complete contrast to the quiet domestic scene inside the house, the outside now erupted with the sound of horses' hooves and wagons as the townspeople returned to dig the grave and attend the funeral. Hamilton and McBeth were there, but the deputy and several of the men had started early on the road to try to find the dog and the trail of the raiders.

The two younger girls were kept inside the house and attended by one of the town women, while the large group stood at the head of the open grave and prayed for the soul of their departed friend and neighbor. Eliza couldn't help but realize the irony of the situation. They hadn't tried to be friendly while the man was alive, leaving him to struggle alone on the farm after the death of his wife with his three young girls as his only companions. She noticed the whispers and the secret speculation about her situation in their eyes while they pretended to grieve. After a last singing of a popular hymn, the group moved indoors, while the men who had volunteered for the duty filled the grave with the brown dirt from which it had been dug.

Eliza spoke to everyone, passing out the food that had been brought by the women, but she couldn't eat. No one dared to ask the question that hung in the air. Finally, their curiosity only half satisfied, the townspeople and neighbors departed, no doubt to gossip as they saw fit, in tight corners or in the town's bars and saloons. Bertha Carson and Mary Louise Stimson left with the others, having been close to the source of the trouble and needing to return to their homes after a twenty-four-hour stay at the farm.

*****

No one noticed the absence of the sheriff from the funeral service. He had taken Eliza's letter to her uncle to the stage coach office, knowing something would need to be done for the children, and there was no time to waste.

On the way in, he took in the devastation. He pulled up his reins at the church, seeing what the darkness had covered in the night. The right side of the window that was the pride of the town was hanging by the leading, near enough ready to fall right out.

"Damn fool brutes," he grumbled. He jerked the reins to get the horse moving, and he let his eyes take in the bank. There was the banker, Hiram Quay, in his fancy gray-striped suit with his half-cut waistcoat and his voluminous side whiskers, moaning in the street, with no one to comfort him. The bank's sign lay on the ground beside him, and broken shards of glass glittered in the sun.

"Sheriff," a voice called. He looked to see Jesse Dukemanier, the town shoemaker and cobbler, angrily striding

160

his way in dark gray pants, unpolished shoes, a woolen, long sleeve shirt, and a bare head. He was followed by two women, Clary Jefferson, occasional seamstress, with her younger sister, Cynthia, holding her tartan skirts out of the dust stirred by her feet, but with a black expression on her face. She wore a ruffled blouse, one that had three buttons instead of two.

"Yes, Jesse?" The sheriff sighed, resigned to the man's confrontational stance. They'd been at odds for years over a dispute about the land title on which his shop resided. The original deedholder had died intestate, with no one to transfer the deed, and Jesse had never been able to get full title to the property.

"Are you letting this happen like this, and not doing nothing?" Jesse shook his fist at the sheriff, spitting his words.

"I agree, Sheriff." Cynthia, the second woman, wearing a deep green dress, with white sleeves and an open weave, and a flowered hat, half simpered and half threw the words as an accusation. "I could've been the one they ravished. We heard about the Jennings' child. Horrible." She shivered but didn't seem so much horrified as envious.

Before he made it to his office, the sheriff faced down three other dissenters and a crowd of about fifteen that had gathered at the saloon. They included Willie Smith, from the butcher shop, wearing trousers stained with blood; Louis Dantin, local minister, looking like he'd been up and ready for just this occasion, in his formal minister's attire, with his stiff black clerical collar and round spectacles; and Solomon Nichols; George Daniels; and Joel Harrington, the county land agent, all in various stages of dress, but decent enough. He calmed them with his soft manner and reassuring voice, though he was certain he would be impeached after this fiasco, if anyone else would take the job.

Once in his office, he sat at his desk to read the girl's detailed observations of her encounter with the outlaws. He was shocked and angry. If he had the raiders in his jail, it would be hard for him to restrain himself from killing them on the spot.

He was still in his office when a little after noon, a messenger ran from the telegraph office with news that the robbers and murderers had been caught by a troop of Union Cavalry about sixty miles south of Crofton. Most of the men, still with the sacks of loot and animals that they had stolen with them, had been killed in the battle that erupted with their capture, and those who survived were quickly hung from the trees of the forest. No one in the town of Crofton was heard to object to this harsh ending to the raiders. War was war, and these men had left too much suffering and loss of property behind them to warrant compassion or sympathy. About half of the horses were returned to the livery stable owner, and the others distributed among the farmers and townspeople from whom they were stolen. The cow and the chickens from the Jennings' farm were never found, and it was determined that the men had eaten them, or they had been stolen by other bandits.

The news of the capture spread throughout the area for a hundred miles as a warning to others who might be tempted to follow their example and prey on unwary civilians. Union troops continued to roam the area for several months, but more pressing engagements took them further afield. Peace and tranquility seemed to settle on the community, and life returned to its normal pattern of hard work, occasional laughter, and Sunday afternoons spent around a good meal.

— 3 —

A meeting of the town council was called to determine what to do with the three Jennings orphans. For over an hour, the discussion went back and forth. The mayor, Percival Randle, in his city-ordered suit of finely woven wool, with a black string tie and polished shoes that seemed to blind anyone who looked too closely, stood and banged his gavel.

"We must have order." He cleared his throat and shifted his oversized stomach inside his wide trousers. He shaped his long moustache with one hand, while looking from under bushy brows at the throng. "A disaster has occurred in our town, and not just in our town, but on the Jennings' farm. We must deal with this fairly and justly, for all concerned. The children should come first. Polly, I believe you wish to speak."

"I do." Polly Finnigan stood. She wore a broad organza

hat with a white fabric flower gracing the crown. Her dress rustled as she shifted her position to face the raised platform and to still be able to speak to those gathered around. "I'm sure there are families that need the help the younger girls can provide, but I'm not sure the elder will be suitable. She would be unmarriable, in any case, with the atrocity that's become her."

As the discussion continued, it came out that one or two childless couples of the area were willing to take in one of the younger girls, but not both. Mrs. Travers, the boarding house proprietor, in her prim navy corset and plain skirt, agreed. Two children would be far too much trouble for anyone to consider. The woman's face was flushed, and she shifted her ruffled yellow collar back and forth to counter the heated discussion warming everyone's blood. No one volunteered to take Eliza, although she was only thirteen years of age. As Mrs. Finnigan suggested, she was now seen as unclean by the highly bred ladies of the town.

With a maturity beyond her years, Eliza argued vehemently that the sisters shouldn't be separated and said that her uncle and aunt would soon arrive to give them solace and security, if the town would be patient until then. The discussion moved on to the land and the farm. Eliza again took up the cudgel. She said that her father owned the land outright. There was no mortgage on it. It was, therefore, the property of her and her sisters, as his only heirs. The town elders complained that their businesses should be given priority and began arguing among themselves. Solomon Nichols and George Daniels eyed Eliza with some interest from their seats in the room. Solomon was a portly man, with thin legs and a clean-shaven, round face. His striped jacket would hardly close, straining the buttons at his waist. He wore black gloves, an affectation, telling of his singular interest: himself. He'd never married, but the gleam in his eye suggested he was considering otherwise.

George was less interested in the marriageability of the girl and seemed to be calculating her value as an investment. The farm was known to have been quite prosperous in previous years, though her father's drink after the death of his wife had caused it to suffer. Extended cuffs from his coat sleeves bore burnished fasteners, and he toyed with them. His collar was tall and stood upright, offsetting his long, thin neck. He swallowed, and his Adam's apple bobbed in his throat. He looked into the room, finding Mrs. Daniels at the back, and nodded once to her. A smile flickered across his face.

The meeting adjourned with nothing settled.

Sheriff Micah Robertson, frustrated and angry over the treatment of the sisters, took the girls to their home and made sure that they had food and plenty of firewood and supplies. He rode by on patrol every few days to see that no fresh tracks of bandits or wild animals were around the farm. The local men decided to leave the blackened ruin of the barn as it was until Clyde Jennings arrived to make decisions. The whole town was certain that he would put the place up for sale, and the bidding was already secretly started for the farm.

*****

Immediately upon receiving the notice from Eliza that

his brother had been wantonly killed on his own front step, Clyde Jennings sold his interest in the general store in which he worked, put his house up for rent, and packed their belongings for the trip to Crofton, Missouri. He and his wife, Augusta, missed the meeting of the town council by five days, arriving on the afternoon stage coach on a Friday in a cloud of dust. If he had attended the meeting, the council wouldn't have argued nor secretly bid for his brother's property, for Clyde Jennings was a very wealthy and powerful man in St. Louis. As soon as he dropped from the coach in front of the freight office, he took charge of the situation. He bought the best wagon that the livery had to sell, two mules to pull it, and three saddle horses. If he'd known these were the same horses that had been stolen by the raiders and returned to their owners, it wouldn't have made a difference in the price. He knew the value of the animals and paid the premium for them.

He told Augusta to wait for him at the small restaurant near the hotel and refresh herself after their long journey, and he drove the wagon to the general store. He picked and plucked at the merchandise as one who was accustomed to the very best products, then bought what supplies he thought necessary to keep the family in comfortable circumstances until he decided on his next move. He left the wagon at the store to be filled with his purchases and walked the short distance to the bank. He asked the manager of the bank if any funds were due from his brother's estate, and when told that Thurston Jennings had owed no money to the bank or the store, he promptly put on deposit enough funds to carry the family through the winter months ahead.

He left the manager of the bank in something of a state of shock, for the poor man never seen so much money deposited in one account on the same day since he'd taken up the occupation of banker in his youth. Since he and his wife had been one of the couples willing to take in a Jennings daughter, the word soon reached the whole town, and the townspeople gaped with astonishment at the news.

Clyde wanted to talk to the Law officer and find out more details about the raid on the town and the slaughter of his brother but was told the sheriff was out of town on business. The deputy was reluctant to speak of the matter without permission from his superior. Clyde, disappointed but resigned to wait until a later date, walked to the restaurant and found his wife finishing a cup of tea and a small iced cake. He bellowed that he needed something more substantial than that and was soon chomping on a thick ham sandwich and drinking a cup of hot, strong coffee.

After their comfortable rest and repast, the couple walked to the general store, where Augusta bought some dolls, drawing materials and colored pencils, and ribbons for the girls' hair, for she knew that Clyde wouldn't think of such frivolous items. She chose some cherry balls and a couple of licorice sticks and, at the last moment, noticed some new canning jars on a table display. She oohed and awed at the size of them and bought them, too. While she was engaged in this maneuver, Clyde demanded from the store proprietor a map to his brother's farm.

The wagon stood loaded and ready to go. Clyde motioned for the livery man to bring the horses and helped to secure them to the back of the wagon. He climbed into the driver's seat and flicked the whip over the tails of the mules. They left town in a dust cloud, amid the whispers and gossiping of many surprised tongues. As soon as he had passed the last saloon and the residential area of town, he turned to his wife, who was laughing in her handkerchief.

"Well, husband, I'm sure the town won't treat our nieces with the usual behavior toward a poor farmer's daughters again. You know that Thurston was a modest fellow, not bent on flaunting his wealth as we've just done before the eyes of the townspeople. He always lived quietly and alone after Rachel's death. The people probably never knew he could call on his resources if necessary in times of drought or the failure of his crops. I hope our actions haven't turned the people against us, while we decide what's best to be done." She sniffed at the dust as they approached an isolated house on the road next to a disused corn field. The large clapboard house hunkered next to the scorched patch of earth. The rain of a week ago that had soaked the ground was gone as if it had never happened.

Once they drew closer, the whitewashed siding revealed chips and overdue repairs. One pillar on the wide front porch sagged slightly, pulling the structure to the left, as though abandoned and tired. The two windows on the opposite side of the house winked brokenly, their eyes half shut. A dormer in the weathered cedar roof revealed an attic or upper story under the slanting structure. It was an impressive home, even in its decay. A red-brick chimney thrust like a flagpole through the roof's peak, a fist shouting defiantly at the sky. The corner of a screened porch hinted at a larger expanse across the back, a memory of summer evenings and family gatherings; but the acre surrounding the building was overgrown, and only a portion of the rear porch could be seen.

He slowed the horses as he gazed curiously at the house, clucked to his team, and they moved more quickly along the road.

"It's well that we keep to our plan, Gussie, for the girls are bound to suffer from the actions of a few cruel women. And, especially, Eliza will receive the slings of gossip and disdain of her neighbors. I fear the girl's mind might be affected by recent events." He kept the team moving at a steady trot so the horses trailing behind could keep up the same speed.

"She didn't seem to be unduly upset in her letter. She seemed calm and wrote of her worry for her sisters, not herself. But, she's always been like her father in that respect. Thurston was never one to grow agitated over the hard life he lived. Even after Rachel's death, he continued to raise the children without the aid of a woman. I suggested he hire a housekeeper, but he said he could care for the girls much better than a stranger could."

"Yes, you're right. I've often envied Thurston's calm acceptance of life's hard blows. For you know I've no patience with that side of the business." Just ahead he saw what he imagined was his brother's farm, and he slowed the animals to a walk to help cool them down.

"There's the place just ahead, I believe, on the right side of the road. It's as Thurston described in his letters. Yes, I can see why the raiders chose this place, rather than the ones we've passed on the way. It's much more prosperous looking, and, except for the loss of the barn, would tempt a group of lawless men to stop and steal the animals.

See the house? And, Rachel's flowers no doubt are still as she planted them, ready for the warmer weather. Remember, Gussie, how Rachel loved the roses and insisted that she have some about her, even in the wilderness?"

Clyde glanced at his wife and found the shine of tears in her eyes. She dabbed at them with her handkerchief. The last time they'd seen Thurston and Rachel was when Eliza was a child of seven before her parents had decided to move to the wilder country. Thurston had hated the thought of civilization encroaching on his property. Clyde clucked to the team and moved them off the road onto the yard of the farm. Before he came to a complete stop, the door was thrown open, and a young slender woman came out. She gave a "Hallo" shout and pointed to the side area under a cluster of trees to park the wagon in the shade.

The uncle and aunt were amazed at the girl's likeness to her father; Eliza had grown winsome and lovely of face, although now showing signs of the bruising she had received at the hands of the villains. Her face was already roughened by the dry winds and hot sun in which she'd worked with her father in the fields at plowing time and at the harvest. Her father had been a large man with broad shoulders, dark hair and eyes, and a sun-roughened face, the perfect example of a farmer. Working as he had with his hands in the harsh glare of the sun all day, he had no softness about him. Augusta was amazed that he had maintained the strength and will to raise his daughters alone. But, Eliza, now, she was his shadow. If she'd been a boy, the resemblance couldn't have been more striking. Tall, with broad-set shoulders for a female so young, her only softness was in her eyes, which were a clear gray.

Eliza's hands were red, for she'd just removed them from a pan of hot sudsy water, when she saw the wagon move into the yard and recognized her visitors. She didn't remember meeting them, but she had gazed often at their pictures, and there was enough of her father in Clyde that she knew him on sight.

She stood and watched as the couple alighted from the wagon, then ran with a moan into Augusta's waiting arms. She held tightly as though she would never let her go. But, hearing the sounds of her stumbling sisters behind her, she drew away and turned to them. They stopped and stared at the man and woman. They had seen many strangers in the last week, but none so foreign in looks and nature. These were indeed city dwellers, dressed in the finest that the merchants of St. Louis could provide. The girls were awestruck.

Eliza motioned for them to come forward, and they moved to obey her, shy and unsmiling.

"These are our family, darlings, come to stay with us awhile. This is your uncle Clyde, who is Father's brother, and this is your aunt Augusta, his wife." She would have gone on with the explanation, but Margaret, the elder, blurted out her pain and sorrow.

"Our papa died and went to heaven with Rastus our dog. 'Liza said he couldn't be found after the barn burned. It was a big fire. I saw it from my window, and we hid in the clothes, while the mean men scared Eliza and hurt her." Her eyes were swimming with tears, and she couldn't go on.

Clothilda, to whom the dog was the dearest, held tight to Eliza's hand. "We heard Rastus crying, and he ran out-

172

side to the barn. We never saw him again. The tall man who came said he ran away, but I think the mean men took him with the cow and chickens. Maybe they ate him."

Clyde could tell that his youngest niece had an imagination as big as she was. He came closer, lifted the child into his arms and swung her high over his head. She let out a blood-chilling scream of excitement. He lowered her to her feet, and she ran to Eliza for protection. He laughed.

"I think the dog just ran away. Some dogs are afraid of fire, you know. Most animals are afraid of fire. He'll come back when he's ready, you'll see." Clyde hoped he wasn't giving the girls false hopes.

"Really? Rastus will come back?" It was Eliza who was looking at him with hope in her eye, for she truly believed that the dog had been killed by the raiders.

"Well, now, Clyde, you shouldn't tell the girls something you cannot promise will come true. You take care of the supplies in the wagons and the animals, while I get acquainted with my nieces." She started toward the door of the house.

Clotilda gripped Eliza's hand tightly. "Eliza, please. What's the missus going to do with us?" Her eyes shone with fresh excitement.

"She's our aunt, and he's our uncle. And, we are their nieces. That means we're family, all of us together, a family who loves and cares for each other, no matter what happens."

Augusta, walking ahead a few steps, was amazed at the insight Eliza showed for one so young. She smiled at the thought of her nieces. She loved children, and she missed her own already, but now she had her nieces to care for, and she would take the opportunity to enjoy every minute of it, for it wasn't at all settled whether they would sell the farm and go back to St. Louis before winter set in. It was up to Clyde to decide what should be done, for it was natural that he was now their guardian, even if the Law hadn't provided him with the legal responsibility.

She opened the door as though it were her own home and walked into the clean, neat kitchen, even as she noticed the bare floor, log walls and the stark usefulness of the primitive furniture and utensils. She removed her hat and gloves and draped her wool cape across the chair. She saw that Eliza had been washing up after a meal. The stove was burning hot and steady, and she smelled the scent of hot chocolate, for the girls wouldn't be old enough to drink coffee.

"What can I do to help? That's what I've come for, you know." Augusta stood poised to help in any way.

Eliza took a deep breath and shooed her sisters into the other room, telling them to play with their toys until she finished the washing up. She turned to Augusta with an expression of hopefulness in her eyes.

"Bread," she breathed, in barely more than a hopeful whisper.

"Bread?" Augusta looked at her niece with surprise in her dark brown eyes.

"Yes, please. That's the one thing that I can't do well. I can make biscuits or cornbread, or fried corn pone, but somehow the bread doesn't rise, or puffs up too high and runs over the side of the pan. I would love a good, wonderful slice of bread with butter and honey. Of course, we have no milk or butter now, for the raiders stole our cow.

174

But we have honey!" She ran to the larder and pulled out a jar half full of the sweet, golden, thick honey. She held it up for her aunt to see.

Augusta laughed. With no further words between them, Eliza found the ingredients her aunt would need, finished washing the dishes and put them away. She took the woman's hat, gloves and cloak into her father's room away from the danger of flying flour and greasy lard. She checked on the girls and brought them back to the kitchen. While her nieces hovered over her shoulders and sat at the table with awe in their glances, Augusta measured and stirred and sifted, and pounded out the dough for three loaves of bread, after ascertaining that there were enough containers for them. That was how Clyde found them, busily engaged in the making of bread. Margaret had a dab of flour on her cheek and dough on her fingers. Clothilda had a tiny piece of dough that she was rolling out, feeling important and loved once more.

He carried in a large wooden box full of the supplies he'd bought at the store in town. Eliza or one of the other girls showed him where to put them, and the luggage and other boxes and bags and barrels from the wagon soon found their places. With each item, the eyes of the three girls grew larger. The house soon became filled with the things the uncle and aunt had brought. Eliza ran to strip her father's bed and put fresh clean sheets on it. She put flannel cloths on the rack on the side of the table that held the clay pitcher and wash basin. She was overwhelmed with the generosity of her relations. Soon the smell of rising dough permeated the house, and it brought back memories of when her mother was alive. She burst into tears and ran from the house.

She didn't know where she was going or why, just running from her emotions. She fled to the pasture, not noticing the three new saddle horses grazing on the verdant grass. She jumped over the rock fence and continued parallel to the road towards town. Micah Robertson came over the ridge, not recognizing and surprised to see the young girl running across the field in a gingham dress. He pulled his horse to a stop and gazed in wonder at the sight. Her skirts were flying with the wind, and her dark brown hair was flowing down her back with abandon.

Finally, Eliza noticed the horseman that had stopped and was staring at her. She paused and pulled her apron up to her cheeks to dry the tears. It seemed to be a signal, for the man urged his horse to come closer. It was then that Eliza recognized the sheriff on his faithful bay stallion. She waited for him to approach.

"What's this, Miss Eliza? Is there danger? Where are your sisters?" He sat still on his horse, looking toward the house and the blackened area that once was a barn. He saw nothing wrong.

"Oh, Sheriff Robertson. It's my uncle and aunt arrived from St. Louis, and she was making bread for us and it . . . it . . ."

"Yes, what did they do? Did they harm you?" He pulled hard on the reins, ready to ride to the house. But, Eliza hiccupped loudly and began to cry again. He dropped from his horse and took her into his arms. "Eliza, what's wrong? Tell me so that I'll know what to do."

She looked up into his sky-gray eyes and felt something that she couldn't explain come over her. She shivered, for she'd never been held by a man before, except for her father. She drew back in embarrassment, her cheeks red and her eyes still damp with her tears.

"She was making bread dough, and he brought in so many things, boxes and bags and barrels. Oh, the house is full of everything, so many things I've never seen before. And, I smelled the bread rising, and it was like my mama was home again. And, my papa. So, I ran away. Come and see. They've come for us. My uncle and aunt from St. Louis have come. We're a family again."

Micah looked toward the house and wanted to cry himself, for his emotions were as raw as Eliza's. He realized with a sharp pain in his gut that for all her hard work and cheerful nature, she was a child, a child with a woman's heart and body, for the raiders had taught her with cruelty and pain what no girl should know until her wedding night. When he thought of the words she'd written in her details of that night, he wanted to pound on something, to kick and scream with the bitterness of it. He was glad the bandits were dead, for he would have gone after them until either they or he was destroyed.

But, this was a happy day for her, and she wanted to share it with him. He took her hand, lifted her onto the back of his horse and moved down the road toward the house. When he came within sight of the man and woman and two girls standing at the front door, he realized it wasn't the proper thing to do, giving a ride on the horse to a young woman. He halted and helped her down, and she ran for her aunt and uncle, throwing her arms around her aunt.

Clyde Jennings watched as the horseman rode toward the group assembled at the door. As he came closer, he saw the shine of a badge pinned to the man's shirt. It was barely visible under his rough, outdoor jacket, but his face was reassuring. He must be the sheriff who had come upon Eliza the morning after the assault. He looked to his wife, and she seemed to also understand the moment of truth. But, why had Eliza run from the house like that? Had she seen the man coming and run to him? The horseman dropped from the saddle and stood, stiff and wary in front of the group.

"Come in, Sheriff. This is my uncle, Clyde, and my aunt, Augusta, whom I wrote to, and they've come to us, like I knew they would." She couldn't go on, for Clothilda and Margaret interrupted the introductions as they broke from the group and surrounded the sheriff with chattering voices and excited laughs. They each took a hand and led him closer. Their eyes sparkled with glee. They clambered for his attention.

Micah stood with the girls at his side, but his eyes didn't waver from the man who stood there waiting for him. He saw something of approval in the eyes so much like those of Thurston Jennings, and he knew that everything would be all right for the girls now. He could relax his vigil over them. He spoke quietly to the girls, and they released him so he could come forward and shake hands with their uncle.

"Hello, Mr. Jennings. I hope you had a pleasant journey from St. Louis. Mrs. Jennings, Miss Eliza said you've been making bread. Ah, how much I used to enjoy the smell of my mother's fresh bread baking in the oven. I'm afraid the memory was too much for Miss Eliza. She's sorely missed a mother's touch. She's a strong, brave young lady, and I'm glad that she has you to help her raise her sisters." He turned to Clyde, and there was a serious look in his eyes.

"Mr. Jennings, I wonder if I might have a moment of your time while I'm on my way to town. The town council has an interest in the rebuilding of the barn. I'm also interested in your plans for the future of the farm. Please, excuse me, Miss Eliza, Mrs. Jennings, girls. I'm tired and need to get to my office in town." He tipped his hat to the women and turned away. He knew that Clyde would follow him as he moved toward the burnt remnants of the barn, the reins of his horse in his hands. He stopped at the water trough and gave the horse its head to drink in the cool water.

Eliza frowned but didn't protest. She gathered the girls and went into the house. Had she angered him with her rude behavior, hugging him like that? Her arms seemed to still tingle from the contact. The smell of the rising dough greeted their entrance, but she wasn't thinking about her parents now. She could only think of the tall, handsome sheriff, who had been her friend when she needed him.

Augusta also pondered the situation. She would wait until the girls were busily occupied before inquiring further into why Eliza had run from the house in such a rude manner. She lifted the cloth from the dough and decided it had risen enough. She began to throw her fists into the pulpy mass, settling her emotions in the process. She was also tired, having traveled a great distance in the stage coach to come to this house with its secrets and its sorrow. She would be glad when the day was done, and she could sleep beside her wise and thoughtful husband once more.

Micah turned to Clyde when he was sure the horse had drunk its fill of water. He tied the animal to the pole where it couldn't reach the trough. He'd told the family he was tired, but it was more. He was consumed with the weariness of a long, eventful day, for he'd ridden to the next county when he heard rumors that some stragglers from the war were seen in the area. They might not be raiders on the lookout for helpless civilians to rob, but still the land was full of men bent on mischief. Some were deserters from both sides in the war. The Union deserters were as dangerous as the Southern Rebels when they were hungry and wanted food or horses. It was times like this when he felt the weight of the responsibilities of his job heavy on his shoulders. Surely, the war would be over soon, and the land settled into tranquility and peace. The sheriff from the next county had assured him that he would take care of any problems that arose at his end of the road.

The two men stood for a time not speaking, as they looked at the blackened timbers and joints of the burnt barn. The smell of the scorched and tortured boards tarred the air with an odor that Micah thought would stain the soil even after the detritus was removed and buried. After a time, the older man shifted his position and cleared his throat, and Micah began to speak.

"I suppose you would like more details from the raid. I didn't know what had happened here until the next afternoon, for they hit the town hard. You might have seen some of the damage as you rode in on the stage coach. Several businesses were burned, and about two dozen horses stolen. I gathered a posse together, and we rode out after them, but we were too late, for while we were collecting the horses still available to us, and getting weapons and ammunitions, they had killed Thurston Jennings and violated his daughter, more than one of them by all accounts. If they had known about the two little ones hiding, they might have been injured, too. I don't know. I often sit and try to imagine what goes on in the mind of men like them, but it's a useless waste of time.

"We headed in a more southeasterly direction, never thinking that they wouldn't travel down the main road; too much of a chance of detection to come this way. My mistake. I take the full blame, for it was my decision to travel the other way. If I hadn't, maybe we would have come in time to save your brother. I believe he lived for a time, several hours even, before he was taken by the elements as much as the bullet wound. It was a dark, cold night. Icy rain and sleet were falling, and the horses faltered in the slick mud."

He paused a moment to collect his thoughts. He didn't look at the older man, for he didn't want to see the condemnation and pain in his eyes.

"After so much rain, it was useless to try to follow them further. The tracks had disappeared, but I left my deputy on the search, and the rest of us came back. It was still raining when one of the men spotted Jennings lying on the step as we rode by. It was fortunate, I suppose, that he was found when he was. It might have been days before Miss Eliza was in any shape to seek help. It's my feeling that she might not have attempted it at all but buried her father herself and kept her own injuries a secret. You've seen some of the remaining bruises on her face, but she was in a bad condition, lying in a pool of her own blood.

181

One of the men beat her with his belt and buckle, and almost bit off her ear."

He couldn't go on for a moment, hoping that the uncle's imagination would carry the picture for him. He took a deep breath and plunged back into the tale.

"I worry that the physical injuries aren't the worst of it. As she lay semi-conscious, she could hear her father calling for help. It lasted all night before he finally succumbed to his pain. Not only herself, but the younger girls, as well. I'm not sure what they heard or saw. They won't talk of it. Two of my posse stayed behind with me through the night, in case the men returned or the girls were injured in a worse way than we thought. To tell the truth, I didn't think Miss Eliza would live through the night. I admire her strength and courage. She wrote it all down for me so it could be used in a trial, but the bandits were captured by the Union troops and made to pay for their sins with their own lives."

Again, the sheriff stopped speaking, his own vengeance coming to the front of his mind. He gritted his teeth and cleared his throat. He glanced at Clyde Jennings and saw a look of utter shock on his face. He had grown pale and looked nauseous.

"Here, now. Are you all right? I'm sorry. Maybe I shouldn't have spoken so bluntly. It's not every man who can abide the gruesome details of a horrible thing like this. It's my profession, and I forget that others don't see things as I do."

"I'm all right. It was the shock. Even though Eliza wrote me telling some of the details, she said nothing of her own condition. She didn't mention the men abusing her. I wonder if Augusta suspects it. She's mentioned a few things I couldn't understand. I put it to women's instinct for trouble. How many men? Did Eliza say how many violated her?" It was Clyde Jennings who now had feelings of vengeance in his heart. The look on his face was fierce, and his jaw was clinched in anger.

Micah assessed the situation with his experience of men's cruelty and wickedness, but he didn't think Clyde would actually take out his vengeance on innocent men, just as he himself wouldn't.

"At least four. She knew that many, before she fainted from the pain and shock. The last one was the worst. She thinks there were as many as six or seven raiders. She could hear them in the house, but they were mostly in search of food and horses. They were in a great hurry, for they must have known my posse was out by then." He shrugged. "If only we'd come down the road at that time, we might have saved her."

"Don't blame yourself, or your men. You did what you could. Now, it's my job to help heal the wounds and take the responsibility in hand. We'll stay the winter. I have no immediate plans at home to take us away, unless there's an emergency with my own children or grandchildren, for they'll always come first. But, as my brother's only male relative, it'll be my decision on what's to be done with the girls and the farm. I need to decide about their education and clothing as well. My wife'll know what's best. I thank you for your kindness and your truthfulness." He reached out his hand in friendship and trust.

Micah mounted his horse and left for town, feeling better that he had gotten the worst of his worries off his mind.

It would always haunt him, that he couldn't save Eliza from her ordeal and hadn't found her father in time to ease his last hours, but the uncle was here to take the heavy burden off his shoulders. Once more, as he rode the familiar route to town and to his home, he wondered at the vagrancy of chance. As he passed the farms of Greer, Shelton, and then Minyard, before coming to the houses at the edge of the town, he puzzled why the thieves hadn't stopped at those farms, especially since it was well known throughout the area that Greer kept some mighty fine horses in his stable, better than those in the livery.

Then he considered that Greer had neither wife nor daughters to violate and allowed it might have been the reason after all.

*****

The second day after the arrival of the Jennings couple at the farm, Paris Hamilton showed up to start his duties as hired hand. With the funds that Thurston Jennings had received from his seasonal barley crop, he had hired him for additional help. With the excitement of the family members arriving, Eliza had almost forgotten. Clyde didn't object to his presence, for he knew that many hands would be needed to restore the farm to its former prosperous ideal. For the next two weeks, the men worked hard to clear the burnt timber and trash from the area around the perimeter of the house. It was set afire a second time, the men careful to not let the girls witness the flames, for it would have brought back painful memories. They used the mules and covered the black mound with dark, loamy soil and planted it with sod, hoping that it would have time by the end of summer to grow thick like a green carpet.

When they relaxed at night, however, the two men bristled and squared off like two massive hounds ready to fight. It was Hamilton's drinking, of course, that Augusta couldn't abide. His swearing and political views were unwelcome to Clyde. But, the girls, Clotilda and Margaret, didn't mind. They loved the old man who'd come to their assistance on that dreadful day when their father died. They weren't old enough to understand about war and the differences between the Northern states and the rebellious South. It was Eliza's calm attitude that finally settled the matter. She stood toe to toe with her adult relatives and told them that Paris stayed. Her father had hired him, and only she could fire him. He was an old soldier who'd fought in the War with Mexico and was entitled to his bitterness against the government and the treatment of its citizens.

On the first of the month, Clyde, with Paris giving him directions in the matter of local politics, ordered lumber, nails and doors for the new barn to be created on the site of the last one. This decision almost caused the two men to come to blows, for Clyde was inclined to build the new one farther out from the house, but Paris insisted that the original site was better. The two men walked around and around the location, with Paris explaining why it had been built there in the first place. It sat on a gentle rise away from the creek so there could be no flooding, endangering the occupants and contents of the building. It was far enough away from the house to contain the flies and insects drawn to the tempting horseflesh and the smell of manure, and yet close enough that a man could do his chores even in the heaviest snow storm without getting lost in the whiteout.

It was while they were discussing the site of the new barn that Clyde thought to ask Paris about the abandoned house at the edge of town. He was told that the Thomas Washburn family had lived in it, but they had moved back to Philadelphia when the war started. The next time he could, Clyde drove into town to talk to Joel Harrington, the land agent, about it. He didn't understand why its attractiveness appealed to him. There was something about the isolation that kept it in his mind. He planned with the sheriff and the land agent to meet at the house the next week.

"Yep, Sheriff, I think this place might do fine." Clyde hooked his thumbs in his vest pockets and looked over the whitewashed clapboards, as though seeing them in their heyday finery. He wore his hat tilted on the back of his head, with full trousers of patterned wool that could encompass a larger man generously. His jacket was unbuttoned, and the inside was a green and yellow tartan. His silver watch chain, swinging from an inside pocket, clattered each time he moved. His hair was thin, and wisps of brown struggled to escape his hat around his ears.

The sheriff knelt, picked up a handful of soil and crumpled it in his fist. It spilled through his fingers like talcum powder. He looked to the dissected field of last year's corn, with the husks clattering in the warm breeze, and he stood, making a snorting sound in his throat.

"I'd like to see the foundation before I make that assessment. Maybe test the timbers in the floors. Might be more work than's feasible." The sheriff brushed his hands and started toward the building, his eyes roving over the structure.

"Right, right," Harrington, the land agent, called, catching up. "The windows need glass, but you can see that. The roof, though, not a leak. Not one. Of course, you'll want to replace the missing shutters. There's some in the attic, but I didn't count to see if they're all there. Don't know why not, though."

They were on the porch by then, and the sheriff tried to straighten the leaning post. The wood was rotted at the bottom, and it remained defiant. The door was unlocked, and the hinges cried in protest when they pushed it open. The place smelled of dust and damp.

"Does it have an inside pump?" The sheriff tapped along one wall, listening to the hollow echo. Wallpaper, the design popular from decades before, peeled from the ceiling like overloaded fly paper. The wide trim work was chipped and yellowed, and a thick layer of dust coated everything.

The kitchen pump did work, after being primed. The water came out rusty for several minutes, then ran clear and sweet. In the basement, an open well was discovered. The sheriff dropped in a stone and smiled when it hit water and the wet sound echoed in the cloistered space. The men agreed that the steps would need rebuilt, something two men could do in a day, even if Clyde didn't offer to be one of them.

Exiting though the wide screened porch, they inspected the outhouse. It had two doors, one for males and the other females. The door was missing on the female side, but Clyde assured the sheriff it could be easily replaced. A small creek bordered the property at the back, though there was little water due to the dry conditions all around.

Right on the spot, Clyde told the land agent he'd buy it. The three men rode in the agent's carriage back to town. The sheriff left them, his mind puzzled by the city dweller's decision. He finally shrugged; it was none of his business. Maybe he and Augusta would remain in the area now that they had become acquainted with the neighbors and business owners.

*****

Four men from the local farms and from the town's saloon were hired to build the barn. Before another month had passed, the building stood taller than the original, and it was soon filled with a cow, two dozen chickens and the three saddle ponies. How Clyde Jennings found such fine animals during a war was discussed and debated for years. But, no one questioned his integrity or his methods after the banker's wife let slip how much money he'd deposited in the bank on his arrival in town.

The horses were put to good use, for Augusta loved to ride, and she taught the girls tricks she'd known since her youth. Almost every day when the weather was fine, she spent the morning with the girls. To hear their laughter ring across the fields sent Paris' heart to pounding. They had come to mean more to the old man than he would admit to any outsider.

It was during one of those early rides that Eliza's secret shame came to the attention of her aunt. At first, the woman accepted that Eliza didn't enjoy the horseback rides, but when she found her pale and nauseous about seven weeks after their arrival at the farm, she began to ask questions which Eliza couldn't deny. From the information she derived from her husband and dated back to the time of the death of Thurston Jennings, and the strange changes in the young woman's body, Augusta knew that Eliza was with child, which became more apparent as the weeks passed. It was certain that no one would be able to determine the father of the child, and it didn't matter since all the men were dead at the hands of the Union Army.

"Wife, this presents a new level of difficulty to our problems. The child rarely goes into town, but this won't remain a secret." The elder Jennings was in a quandary, and his worried expression showed it. "Our only solution is marriage, and quickly."

"She's only a child, Clyde. How can we do that to her?" Augusta bemoaned the frustrating but incontrovertible situation. Although Eliza seldom left the farm, she was at the stage where her secret would soon be visible among the inhabitants of the county. The matter could no longer be ignored, as Eliza was rapidly coming to the end of her fourth month in the family way. Even her younger sister, Clothilda, noticed the size of the lump in her belly when she crawled into her lap to be read a nighttime story.

"It's already been done, my dear. The girl is woman enough to bear a child. The best solution to the problem is to find our niece a husband, and without delay." It had been speculated on in the lower regions of town from the beginning, and some of the more progressive ladies of society were counting the months. Clyde didn't mention that to his wife, leaving the matter unsaid.

One night not long after, a fierce windstorm erupted over the farm, and Clyde awoke in the dark with the perfect answer, as though it had blown in with the storm, and he chastised himself for his ignorance. The loud banging of hail on the tin roof of the barn kept him awake, and finally he rose and walked to the kitchen to find something to quiet his uneasy stomach muscles. He unearthed a couple of slices of leftover ham and a hunk of bread and sat at the table, drinking a glass of water. The idea was growing so clearly and silently in his mind that at first he rejected it as a fantasy, and then with a start, he awoke to the real possibilities of it working. He remembered the few times the sheriff had visited the farm since their arrival and the way he inquired after the health of Eliza. Of course, he included the younger girls in his query, but it was the way he looked at Eliza that settled the matter in Clyde's mind. He left the better part of his ham sandwich on the table and roused his sleeping wife with no thought to her discomfort.

Thunder roared outside the house; and the windows were alight with the brilliance of the lightning flashes as Clyde whispered his idea in his sleepy wife's ears. She listened with her eyes becoming ever wider as the idea grew and became a planned action. It was the perfect solution to the problem. They looked at it from every angle; every thought was brought into the open and either agreed upon or rejected as unworkable. They didn't even notice when the two younger girls went into their sister's bed, and the three huddled together, finding solace in each other from their nighttime fears. The storm continued to rage on the outside, while the couple whispered their misgivings if the idea should fail to bring the joy they so hoped would restore harmony in the house.

Nothing was said at the breakfast hour about a trip to town. Clyde Jennings and Paris Hamilton examined the damage to the tree limbs and discussed the shape of the animals, all safely ensconced in the barn. The mules were a little roughed up, having spent the night seeking shelter under the eaves of the vast building. But, with a soothing rub of salve, Paris was sure their hides would recover from the pounding of the hailstones. It was the chickens that worried him. Even enclosed as they were under shelter, they might not lay eggs for a few days, and Paris loved his fried eggs of a morning. He had heard their frantic cackling and hawking all night, for the noise of hail on a tin roof can be frightening for a man, much less a few feathered hens.

With the simple pretext of riding into town to acquaint himself with the possible damage to the neighbor's crops, Clyde rode from the farm as innocent-looking as a new-born lamb. Only his wife knew the real purpose of his visit to the quiet hamlet of Crofton, Missouri. He arrived about mid-morning, it being a Thursday. He left his horse at the livery and walked the short distance to the sheriff's office.

*****

Sheriff Micah Robertson had also spent a sleepless night, but for a vastly different reason. News of the war in the South wasn't good. The raiders from the Southern states or neutral territories were becoming more numerous and bold. Looters had been shot near the border of Missouri and Kansas Territory. As the only peace officer within a radius of fifty miles or more, he was responsible for the safety of his town. The thunder and lightning of the night had kept him thinking of the burning of the Jennings' barn.

What if the raiders invaded his town again? Would he be able to hold them off? Could he save the women and children from a similar fate as that which Eliza had endured?

He broke out in a cold sweat when he remembered her lying on the floor. He rose early from his bed, snatched some warm clothing to cover himself and raced out the door of his small boarding house room. He calmed himself before he reached the front door. It wouldn't do to alarm the other residents of the house. He took his hat and jacket from the peg on the wall and left before the sunrise, strapping his pistol holster and belt on his hip as he walked.

Now, hours later, his alarms of the night seemed childish and panic-stricken. He was glad that no one had seen him at the time. His stomach growled from hunger, for he hadn't stayed for the meal provided by the wonderful Mrs. Travers, proprietor of the boarding house, although he'd consumed at least a quart of coffee from the pot in his office. He lay back in his leather chair, with his booted feet propped on the desk, half asleep and wondering whether he should hire a few more deputies, one to help Potter patrol the town, and maybe a few to patrol the rural areas of the county, when he heard the opening of the office door. He slammed his feet to the floor and rose almost at the same time, alert to any danger. He placed his hand near his holster but withdrew it when he saw that his visitor wasn't hostile.

He grinned sheepishly at Clyde Jennings as the man started forward, his hand outstretched and a smile on his face. His palm was as soft as a babe's cheek to the touch, and Sheriff Robertson was surprised, for he knew the man had worked hard at the farm during the unforgiving months of the spring planting season.

"Good morning, Sheriff. I hope I find you well after the storm of the night past."

Micah was always amused at the citified way of talking. He was more accustomed to the sound of a farmer's common slang and imperfect usage of the American language. He kept a calm, inert look on his face, however. He was trained in not letting his emotions show on the surface. It could mean the difference in life or death to a man of the Law.

"Ah. Yes, you might say that I'm well enough. I haven't heard the damage reports from the far reaches of the county. The town seems to have suffered no catastrophe." He frowned. "Have you come to tell me that lightning has struck that fine new barn of yours?" It suddenly occurred to him that the man had never visited his office before today. The alarms of the night again took hold of his imagination. Maybe the man had come to tell him of the very thing he'd worried about all night, that raiders were in the area.

"Not a bit of lightning, Sheriff, not that struck the barn. My trees, well." Jennings shrugged as if it didn't matter.

"Is everything all right, then? Is Miss Eliza well?"

Jennings' smile grew wide. "Everything's going well. The animals are thriving. The crops are growing. As I said, a few tree limbs broken off by the wind, oh, and a bit of hail is all the damage we received. It's something more in a personal vein that I want to discuss with you today." He looked around but found no other chairs, so leaned against a tall shelf.

"Personal? What could be personal between you and me?" Sheriff Robertson felt at a disadvantage, although he was the taller of the two men. He could sit in his chair behind the desk and establish himself as an officer of the Law, or he could remain standing, for it looked to be a long conversation. His mind considered they could talk in one of the jail cells, but then he wouldn't be able to see through the windows into the street if trouble arose.

Clyde cleared his throat. "It's about my niece, Eliza. You know the girl, were there the morning after her father was killed. She's told me you were very kind and sympathetic to her cause. You raised a posse and tried to find the murderers yourself." He paused a moment, as if searching for the right words.

"Yes, and the next afternoon to help clean the scene before the ladies of the town appeared." He frowned. Jennings knew all this, for he had told him the facts himself. "What's wrong? You said that she was well."

"Ah. The fact is that her health is excellent, as far as her appetite or any sickness she might have caught. The thing is, Sheriff, the bandits left her with child. I've been at my wit's end trying to come to a solution to the problem."

"A child?" The sheriff jumped as though he'd been gut shot. He grabbed his stomach as though he might be ill himself, and he felt his face grow cold. He'd read Eliza's account of the attack, but he never imagined it might come to this. "But, how can this be? She's only thirteen, not even fully a woman."

"Well, as to how it might happen, I don't know. I've discussed it with my wife. It was only the one time after all, but there were at least four men." Jennings shrugged. "The chances may be slim to none for a child her age, but somehow it happened, and now the problem is about to show itself to the townspeople. With the secret out, she can have no more peace, for they'll hound her and gossip and try to make her out to be a scarlet woman, when it's through no cause of her own that she bears this child, for she is herself an innocent girl."

Jennings stopped talking, for by this time he'd let his anger and frustration come to the surface, turning his face red. He fought to keep himself under control, and he took a deep calming breath.

"My wife and I agree that the best solution is either we get her a husband or send her away. Now, if a man could be found for the right price—"

"You're trying to buy her a husband? How could you think she would agree to that?" It was now Micah's turn to be angry.

"Oh. She'll agree, all right. You don't know her well, if you think she'd reject the idea of a husband and father for her unborn child. Every girl grows up dreaming and planning for the day of her marriage and child birthing. It's just coming a little early in her case. Even old Paris Hamilton would do for a husband, if he would settle down and stop drinking." Jennings laughed out loud, then he caught himself when he saw the quick frown that appeared on the sheriff's face. He blinked his eyes a couple of times and restrained himself.

"You want me to help you find Eliza a husband? Is that why you've come? I know most of the men in the county, young and old. I'd need some time to think about the matter." Micah took a deep breath. He'd never seen or thought of himself as a marriage broker before. He quickly considered the young men in town. There was Potter, his deputy, and James McBeth, the saloon keeper. Both had been there on the night that the killing and raiding had taken place. No. He dismissed the saloon keeper immediately. He wouldn't expose Eliza, a gently bred young woman, to the carousing of drunken men. Potter? No. He wouldn't do, for he was impulsive and liked his freedom too much for settling down for marriage. Jackson he dismissed immediately. At the time of the disaster at the ranch, the man hadn't had the sense to fill a bucket of water. He couldn't raise a child, not until he reached his own maturity. Now, Jesse Dukemanier or George Daniels might agree to such an arranged marriage. But, there were the two small girls to consider, too. A man married to Eliza Jennings would have to take care of the sisters until they were old enough to make marriages of their own. Micah couldn't think of any other men in the area who would be suitable for a husband.

Jennings didn't interrupt Micah in his rambling thoughts but watched as the man came up with himself as an answer. When that didn't seem to be the case, he interjected his own idea of the ideal husband for his niece.

"I was thinking of you as Eliza's husband. She's young, but she's a good homemaker, well trained in cooking, sewing, and the hardship of farming. You're the sheriff now, but soon you'll have to think of your future. You might not be elected again. The townspeople will want a younger man, that deputy, Potter, for instance."

"Potter as sheriff?" Micah laughed, but the idea took hold in his mind. He was twenty-seven years old. He was having trouble with his eyesight. He couldn't depend on his steady hand with a gun, nor a clear eye much longer. It might, indeed, be soon enough that he would have to find another occupation.

A fresh thought hit him hard. Clyde Jennings was willing to buy a husband for his niece. And, she was willing to accept whomever he chose for her. He remembered her warmth as she'd hugged him that one time, and the sparkle in her soft gray eyes when she was happy. A child in years maybe, but with a growing child in her womb, she was without doubt a woman.

He didn't want to be a farmer. He had a small dream of becoming a gunsmith. He knew about weapons of all kinds. He read the most recent journals about the repeating rifles, and pistols that could carry bullets in a clip rather than fire one at a time. Would it be possible that he could open a gunsmith shop in Crofton and retire with an easy life? His inner conscience rejected the idea of payment, but if he was to take on the duties of husband and father of an unknown outlaw's child, and caretaker to the other two girls, he'd need an occupation to support the family. The frown turned to a smile of anticipation, and he leaned in closer, as though the very walls of the jail might tell the world his secret.

"How much? How much are you willing to pay a man

to marry your niece and become father to her unborn child?" The sheriff felt his breath quicken with the possibilities, for Clyde Jennings was well known to be a wealthy personage.

*****

Clyde was astonished at the question, for of all the men he'd met, he wouldn't have believed that this man would truly desire a payment for marriage in kind. He was willing to pay a great deal to have the matter settled, so he and Augusta could go back to their personal lifestyle, the life they had chosen for themselves, and to be near their children and grandchildren in Kansas City, but the shift in tone carried greed, and that unsettled him. Clyde took so long to answer that Micah began to backpedal.

"Of course, you wouldn't want a Law officer daily engaged in a dangerous line of work to marry the girl and raise her child. What if he were mortally wounded in the line of duty? What if he tried to stop the raiders and was killed? That's me, you realize, my job, what I'm elected to do." He shuddered, for the idea wasn't a new one. "I might die young, and Eliza still wouldn't have a father for her child."

"One thousand dollars in gold, or, in government script, if you prefer." Clyde refused to let this opportunity slip away, and he upped the ante. "And, I'll throw in that house at the edge of town we saw. Free and clear, no mortgage. On the day you sign your name to the marriage papers and speak your vows, the money will be deposited in your name in the bank. Also, I'll add a certain annuity for each year the marriage lasts. One year after the wedding, one thousand dollars; two years, one thousand more; until the child is of age, in which case the money will go directly to him. If additional children are born, the price will increase as the sex is determined. More for a male child, of course." Clyde smirked and winked his eye.

"Him? You know the sex of Eliza's child already?" Micah frowned, the presumption not sitting well with him. Future children were indeterminate, but for one in the womb? No one could foretell that.

"It's what my wife has decided. My niece will surely agree. Whether it will be so or not, heh. What comes is what comes."

"One thousand, you say." Micah was heady with the prospect, and he felt a wave of dizziness behind his eyes.

Clyde watched as the respected sheriff of Claymore County, Missouri, reeled back and fell into his leather chair behind his desk from shock, his face stiff and pale as a snowflake. He knew then that he could have set a much smaller amount. He was satisfied with the chance he and Augusta had taken. There was one more stipulation that he must make. While Micah was still in shock, he demanded the sacrifice of human frailty.

"Of course, the marriage must take place immediately, to save the girl embarrassment with the child advanced in the womb. You know the county clerk and will be able get the certificate today. I believe there's a minister of the gospel in town. Summon him to meet us at the farm tomorrow. If you fail to show up, I'll cancel all arrangements and swear that the offer was never made between us. One final thing, the marriage must be consummated as soon after the wedding ceremony as possible. I insist on it or no money will change hands."

Once the commitment was made, Micah was too honorable a man to back down. He stood up, walked around his desk and shook hands with his future uncle-in-law. Left between them was the unspoken promise. After the wedding service, he would be lord of the manor and king of his own estate. His decision on all marital matters were his alone and final, with or without the consent of the bride. It was the tradition of the times in which they lived. Clyde would no longer have control over her destiny.

Clyde and the sheriff, having made their business arrangement, were now ready to put their plan into action. They walked out the door, leaving it unlocked as usual, for Potter would be there soon to take over the night duty. Still in something of a daze, Micah walked beside the other man to the courthouse, greeted his friends, nodded at those he didn't know, and filled out a legal form of matrimonial bondage between himself and his proposed bride, Elizabeth Ann Jennings. He put the signed copy in his pocket, shook hands with Clyde and moved on down the street to the southwest toward the home of the protestant minister of the gospel, explained the urgency of the date of marriage, received a reply and went home.

*****

Micah didn't eat that night, nor did he sleep well for the second night in a row. There was a feeling of heaviness in his midsection, as though he'd consumed a large meal and it hadn't digested well. He awoke from a half-sleep in the darkness of his room, his body longing for rest, and went over again the facts of the raid on the town and the Jennings' farm. He rose in something of a panic, for he didn't even remember the girl's face; only the white form of her crumpled body and the blood that covered it.

Suddenly, those things were important. Could he take her in his arms and make her his wife forever? Could he lie beside her every night knowing that at least four men, maybe six had known her in the Biblical way? Micah Robertson, the man, not the courageous sheriff of the county, grabbed his stomach and rushed outside to the darkness, in time to lose what small amount of ingredients were left from his lunch. He heaved until his face was sore from grimacing, his stomach ached and his hands were shaking from the upheaval. He fell to his knees in the cool, damp night air, and for the first time since he was a child prayed to the heavenly Father above to make him worthy of Eliza's respect.

— 4 —

Friday morning dawned bright and clear, with the early sky a dark crimson and gold. The sun rose in the sky as though the events of the previous night were passed and done. Today was a new world, clean, fresh and ready for its own share of troubles. Sheriff Robertson made himself some coffee and forced himself to eat several slices of crisply fried bacon and buttered and toasted bread. He needed the strength, for his hands were still shaky from the night before. He packed enough clothing for two days in his saddle bags, for after the marriage and the consummation of his marital contract, he would have to return to town to continue his duties. If anyone asked he would simply say duty called him away, but no one asked. Word had gotten around town in the wee hours that he was to be married, and several men shook his hand and congratulated him on his good luck. Mrs. Bertha Carson greeted him with her sweet smile, and Micah wondered if she knew the secret.

At the Jennings' farm, the early morning chores were taken care of in the usual way. The hired hands, Thomas Deming and Paris Hamilton, went about their duties silently, but it wasn't for lack of talk. There was plenty to talk about this morning, though neither man dared discuss the consequences of the tragedy at the farm that were beginning to come to light. The older couple, arrived to care for their nieces, was determined to prevent the shame and disgrace of an unwed mother being thrust on the innocent child, as shared the previous evening by Clyde as he told Paris he'd arranged a marriage with Micah Robertson, the sheriff. A glow of satisfaction now rested on the elder Jennings' face. When asked why, Clyde admitted that a child was coming into the household, and he needed a legal name that would be carried with honor and pride.

Inside the house, all was bustle and excitement. The two younger girls, not really knowing what was happening, only that their sister was getting married, were dressed in their best gowns, and Augusta made some silk flowers for their hair from one of her old shawls. The smell of food permeated the house, some giving off a sweet fragrance and some not so sweet. The table was piled high with food, for the women had started cooking and baking when Clyde had returned from town, carrying a smile on his face.

With his hat in hand, fresh from his discussion with the sheriff, Clyde had brushed the dust of the road from his trousers and taken Eliza into the parlor. Outside, the clouds were tinged with peacock colors, telling of the quickly approaching evening. They positioned themselves on two chairs, and he took her hand in his.

"Child, you are well on your way to becoming a woman. You're fully aware you are with child, and the sheriff has agreed to a marriage to give the child a legal name. It's all arranged for the morning."

"Uncle, no!" Eliza turned white at the thought of marriage to the kind, gentle man with the gun at his hip, who had watched over her and came by occasionally to see how she was. She shook with fright.

"What it is, child? He's a good, kind man."

"He will . . . in the night . . ." She broke down with tears in her eyes, pulling her hand away and shaking as she hugged herself tightly.

"You'll adjust, my child. Not all men are like those who invaded your home that rough and horrid evening."

She gasped with shock when Clyde shared that he had offered the sheriff a dowry so that he would accept the child she carried as his own. She trembled with despair when she thought of his occupation and the violence that was his constant companion. But, deep in her heart where only she could see, she rejoiced that he had accepted the offer, even if the bride price might come between them in the future. Marriage, any marriage, was the only alternative to her situation, for she had her two sisters to consider. She couldn't abandon them and pretend that awful night hadn't happened. It had, and the sheriff, more than any other man, would remember all his life his first sight of her on the day afterward. She looked out the window at the glow of crimson and gold of the sky and focused on the fluffy white clouds flung across the horizon. She promised herself and God that she would never complain nor neglect her duty to him. With God's will, she would give him other children, children of his own to have and hold in his heart forever, not one of a murderous outlaw produced in cruelty and lust.

The first visitor to arrive that early morning was the minister of the gospel, Louis Dantin, decked out in his fine wool suit even on a day that looked to be hot and sultry.

"Welcome, all." Dantin moved among the family, shaking hands and greeting the children, but his eyes kept searching out the house, from which emanated the allure of the prepared and aromatic dishes out on display. Perhaps it was his first opportunity to receive a good hot meal in a long time, for he jumped on the food as though he were a starving man, as soon as Augusta, in her duty as hostess, offered him a sampling taste.

"Reverend, my sweet potato pie is the best in the county, I'm sure. Will you concede to approve my skills?" Augusta shifted her collar around her neck and invited him to the house.

"Why, um, I couldn't before the ceremony, could I?" He smiled, pleased, and he moved toward the house alongside Augusta.

"A small amount won't be missed. I made several." Augusta's voice faded away as they entered the domicile.

The man was so thin and emaciated that he looked frightened and haunted, as though the demons of hell were chasing him. Eliza was curious enough to ask him, but not bold enough to embarrass him if it were true.

The second and third carriages contained the ladies who had attended her and her father on that fateful day after the attack, Mrs. Bertha Carson and Mrs. Mary Louise Stinson, with their husbands and a dozen portable chairs from the church hall. She was glad to see them and gave them a hug of welcome, although she hadn't expected them. She'd assumed it would be a quiet, quick affair with few witnesses. Before the women could be settled comfortably in their chairs, other wagons and carriages arrived, plus several single men on horseback and one familiar family in a donkey cart. Soon, the barnyard was full of conveyances of all kinds, and Augusta was moaning in despair, afraid they wouldn't have enough food. There was no need to worry, for each family grouping brought their contribution to the occasion. The table and the countertop almost groaned aloud with the weight of the food. Finally, it was decided between Clyde and the preacher that it would be necessary to take the ceremony outside under the tree because the house wouldn't hold all the witnesses to the marriage of their county sheriff.

*****

Sherriff Robertson arrived midway between the arrival of Mrs. Ava Johannson, the wealthiest citizen of the town, her late father being a coal miner from Pennsylvania, and the carriage carrying the half-drunken "ladies of the night" from James McBeth's saloon, for if anyone believed he would be welcomed this memorable day, it was McBeth, who had comforted and supported the young girls on their most trying day. He wasn't disappointed, nor his "ladies," for he was given a warm welcome by the bride and the groom. Each of the little girls, in their pretty frocks and silk flowers, ran and gave him a hug, and he lifted Clothilda onto his shoulders and swung Margaret around by her hands. They squealed with joy and excitement. The women were introduced to Eliza, and she welcomed them with a sweet smile. The groom frowned but didn't comment. After all, the man was a voter, too. And, their nocturnal occupation wasn't to be condemned on this joyful occasion.

The sheriff was almost overwhelmed by the number of people who had come to the Jennings' farm, but he wasn't dismayed because he knew that some of them came from curiosity, to see where Thurston was killed on his front doorstep and his daughter taken without her will on the floor of her bedroom. The surprise was that Eliza was so pretty and cheerful about the situation, taking her most important day in her stride as though she were welcoming the queen of England to her home.

When the preacher called for attention, Micah felt his heart thump so loudly that he thought it would burst. He stepped forward with a sense of doom and sadness, but he painted a smile on his face and kept it there during the whole ceremony. He repeated his vows with a clear, steady voice, and listened with anticipation for the words that pronounced that they were now husband and wife together, and with God's approval, amen. The word was repeated in many voices, both male and female.

*****

Only at the very last minute did Eliza tremble and lose her courage. She could feel the presence of the people behind her; some out of curiosity, some out of political expediency, for the raiders had caused many in the county to lose their possessions and their self-respect. It was perhaps a moment of revenge for them to know that Eliza and the sheriff were made one under God's care. They represented the people of the county, law and order, justice and forgiveness, honor and decency, in a world torn apart by madness and war.

Amen. Let it be so, the Bible says.

But, on that clear day in July, the sounds of war were far away. She self-consciously placed her hand on her stomach, where the baby, conceived in lust and greed, awaited his time to live.

"Dear Heavenly Father," she began a silent prayer, "Please that he might grow up in a world at peace, neighbor with neighbor, country with country."

As Clyde had predicted, Eliza had already decided the child would be male. She felt tears come to her eyes. It was a futile gesture, she knew, and that was when she lost her courage, for standing beside her was a man of violence and greed. She would never forget that her uncle had paid him to share his name with her child born of cruelty. She repeated her vows with acceptance, for at least the child would bear the name of a man known to her, despite his faults and frailties.

"Micah, do you take this woman . . ." the preacher started, and Eliza felt her head swim with the upcoming portent of the expected answers. In a daze, she heard the sheriff agree, and the preacher turned to her.

"Eliza . . ." She heard nothing else and simply nodded her head when the thin man's mouth stopped moving.

As soon as the vows were spoken, the men drifted towards the door to the kitchen where the food was laid out, or else to a certain wagon, where it was made known that some bottles of liquor were kept. The women stood for a while longer, sharing the moment, for they didn't have many chances to communicate with each other, and removed to the kitchen to restore order as they passed out plates piled high with food and utensils.

Eliza saw the events of the day unfolding around her, and yet, she wasn't certain she would remember any of it.

*****

Of all the people present that day, it was perhaps the groom, himself, who felt the occasion held a forecast of the future, for he had received a notice early that morning from the telegraph operator that some Confederate troops had been seen fifty miles away, heading north toward them. And, from the north, heading southeasterly, were additional Union cavalry troops. If they happened to meet in this area, it would be chaos and trouble for everyone.

Sheriff Robertson laughed at the men's jokes, told some of the guests to lay off the liquor, lest they force him to slam them into his jail; and others he told to hurry home before dark, for it wasn't safe on the roads during a war. He smiled and shook hands. He played cheerfully with the children who approached him, and at last the crowd began to move away as the evening progressed. He breathed a sigh of relief when he saw James McBeth and his women leave in peace with their critical neighbors.

He paid the minister a small token and promised he'd think about bringing the new missus to worship service. He saw Paris Hamilton give him a look of worry and dread, and he questioned him, although the look was clear.

"So, Paris, what's that sour look I see?" Micah said the words lightly, as if to laugh it off.

"I see your shoulders, and they don't carry the stance of a man looking forward to his wedding night. What news have you of surrounding events? A war is going on, though it's not here just now. It could be, with little warning. Should we be preparing the farm for intruders?"

"Have no worries. All's well," but he wasn't sure, himself. "Let's make the most of this day and not let tomorrow's trouble intrude."

Paris snorted as if he didn't quite believe it, but he didn't continue the discussion. At last, everyone except the hired hands were gone, and Micah was alone with his new relatives. It felt strange that he had family again after so many years. His parents had died of cholera when he was twenty years old, and he had roamed the western lands and territories, alone and unafraid until the war commenced on his very doorstep, for he'd been in eastern Kansas when the first shots were fired. The worst part of the war wasn't always on the battlefronts of the East, but on the frontier where armed men took the war to the civilian populations at will.

"I must stop these gloomy thoughts. This is my wedding day," Micah said aloud, determined to cast off the worries that nipped his heels.

Still, he worried. Would she reject his advances, out of fear and distrust? She was only thirteen, an age when a maiden should be carefree and gay. Instead, she was a violated woman bearing an unwanted child. Well, no more. From this day forward, he promised himself, this child would be wanted and cared for and loved as any child should be. His wife would be his first consideration, and after that, her child and his chosen occupation. He wasn't surprised when Clyde told him to come to the corral to see his new acquisition, a black stallion of strength and stamina. There, under the shade of a lowering willow tree, money changed hands, and the two men shook in full agreement that the contract was sealed, and the marriage would soon be consummated.

*****

Long after her sisters had gone to bed, and Augusta had cleaned the kitchen and joined Clyde in their room, Eliza turned her attention to her own affairs. She told herself she wouldn't resist when he came to her. Still, memories of that horrible night remained to haunt and to taunt her with their pain and sadness. Sometimes, she saw the natural red of the sky, and it blended in some strange way with the glow of the fire in the barn. She wondered for a moment if her father would have chosen the sheriff as a life's companion for his daughter. No. He was opposed to all violence and wouldn't have accepted a man of the Law as her husband. She sighed and ran her brush through her long, dark hair. She hated the length of her hair and wished she had the courage to cut it short. She laughed a bit to think of Augusta's reaction to that.

It was the laughter that Micah heard as he approached the bedroom door on anxious feet. How could she laugh when she slept each night in the same bed where she'd been dragged out and violated, he wondered? How could she bear to think of the child inside her when it was conceived in such a manner? He opened the door softly and entered. He wasn't quite sure of the proper procedure for a husband to approach his wife on her wedding night, so he'd waited until he hoped she was in bed and covered from top to toe, but she was seated at the table, with the brush in her hand, softly chuckling over her private joke. He walked toward her, and she smiled.

"What's funny, my wife? Do you think this day was so pleasant that you can pass it off with a private joke?" He took the brush from her hand and began to slide it through her long hair with ease, for she had already brushed all the tangles from it. He touched it with his left hand. It was soft and silky to the touch. He leaned down and smelled the fragrance of violets. Where did she find violets, in the wilderness of Missouri?

"It's my hair."

"Your hair's funny?" Micah was so pleased with the softness of his wife's hair that he had almost forgotten his question.

"I was thinking of the expression on my aunt Augusta's face if I cut it short, like yours, maybe. It would be so funny to see her shocked at the sight of a woman with clipped hair."

"Why would you want to cut your hair, my lady? It's lovely, especially in the softened light from the lamp." Micah took another whiff of the violet silk. He leaned in and kissed the top of her forehead. It was the first time he'd touched her except for the clasping of hands during their wedding service since the morning he found her weeping about some bread dough. He refused to glance to the spot where she'd lain injured on the floor, even though it was only feet from where he now stood.

"I hate my hair long. It's hard to wash and takes hours to dry. Sometimes I get a headache from the weight of it. I wish I could have it cut short, like a man's." She sighed and then flinched as the brush that he was wielding drew too tightly against her scalp.

"It's so beautiful, clean, so fragrant. I'd never have you cut your hair, but if it's a problem for you, cut it. I'll stand against your aunt on your behalf. She'll not dare object if your husband approves." This last was said almost in a whisper. He laid the brush on the table top and drew her to her feet. Her eyes opened wide at his advance. She swayed on her feet from the excitement as he drew her gently into his arms.

"Don't be afraid, my pet, for I won't harm you, if I can help it. You're precious to me and alive where once I thought you dead. When I first saw you on the floor surrounded by the horrors of the raider's attack, I thought you wouldn't live through the day, and here you are, trembling in my arms." He took a strand of her hair, drew it to his lips and kissed it, then put it next to her own lips and smiled. "See, darling girl, your hair is for me to adore and play with, not you. It's the husband's privilege to see his wife's crowning glory in disarray about her as she sleeps. But, I have no desire to force you to keep it long if you want it cut. Do what you want from now on. You're mine, after today, and only I have any say in what you do."

Eliza's face burned, and she felt she might cry. "How can you say I'm precious to you, when my uncle's money has paid for you to marry me? How can you hold me close when the child I'm carrying is another man's?" She withdrew her hand from his, placed it across her belly, and looked at him sadly.

He led her to the edge of the bed and sat beside her. He gently kissed her on the lips and took her hand into his and kissed it, too.

"Haven't I said that you're alive when I thought you dead? You're alive, my precious, my golden girl, my Eliza. You're not cold and dead and stiff in the coffin beside your father. You're here in my arms, where you were meant by God's will to be. The money doesn't matter to me. If you want it returned to your uncle, say the word and it's returned. It's not the money I desire, but to hold you close, watch the child grow inside you, and to watch him mature up into a man of stature and honor, unlike his father, who was selfish and cold. I agreed to use the money for you and your sisters' and our children's benefit. I won't always be a sheriff. I'll need a new start; a new occupation. I know very little except how to use a gun and read a law book. I can farm, if that's your desire. I can plow the fields, harvest the grain, and dig a well for water, but that's what I ran away from, my dear. I can do those things if I need to, but it isn't my wish to do them when men like Paris Hamilton and Thomas Deming can be hired to work the farm."

"I understand. I see your intents now. You're looking toward the future, while I'm thinking only of the price my uncle paid for you. If I asked you, would you truly give up your position of power and authority and become a simple farmer? Would you?" Her lovely eyes were anxious as they gleamed in the light from the lamp.

Micah dropped her hands and turned away. He thought

long about what she was asking and decided an honest answer was all that mattered. He turned back and looked into her soft gray eyes as though he would drown in their depths if she asked.

"I don't want to be a farmer. I don't want to plow the fields, nor harvest the crops. To toughen my hands in physical labor is abhorrent to me, but if it'll make you feel safe and wanted, then I'll become a farmer. Tomorrow, I'll go to Judge Mathews and hand him my resignation. It'll take some time before an election can be held, and these are dangerous times, so I might have to continue until another man is chosen by the people."

"No. Don't resign your position. It's my own insecurity I'm thinking of. You're needed by the people. I saw that today. They respect you and, because of you, the Law. Continue in your chosen field until a time is right for us to start anew in another time or place, for I don't want to stay here forever. I've wanted to travel to far places, to see the mountains or the sea since I was a child. Keep the money my uncle offers you. Use it for what you think is best. I'm a selfish girl for thinking of changing you, when it's your character and honesty that drew me to you from the beginning."

"You were drawn to me? Even in your pain and sorrow, you were drawn to me? That makes me humble." His voice changed as he listened to her in disbelief. He looked away and couldn't face her reaction to his words. "I must honestly say that if your uncle hadn't approached me, I'd never have offered for you, nor even considered you for my wife. I never wanted a wife. I wanted to be free to roam at will. But, his arguments were just. His money was tempting. I know that the child needs a father. I'll honor you with my body and my mind until the day we're parted, be it long or short. The child will become my own. This I promise you. I won't desert you nor hurt you if it's in my power."

Softly, and with a gentleness hardly possible in a man with an occupation of violence and danger, he took her into his arms and kissed her. She stiffened at first, as visions of her attackers and the feel of their wet, clammy lips and hands ran through her mind. The cruel assault only months before pressed against her memory, causing her to shiver. She withdrew, and Micah let her go. He looked at her with compassion.

"Shall we wait until you're ready? I won't force you into accepting my advances if you're unsure or feel unsafe. However, I believe that if it's to be done, it would best be done now, for if you wait longer, the memories will grow and grow in your mind, until you won't allow me to touch you at all. I won't go any further than you wish."

Eliza had never known such a man. Her father, whom she had adored, was stubborn and sometimes cruel to his daughters. She knew with a woman's mature instinct that she could trust this man with her life, if need be. Surely, she could trust him with her person. At that moment, Eliza Robertson made the most important decision of her young life. She surrendered herself into her husband's care.

Shyly and with a new insight into womanhood, she kissed him on the lips and drew him into her arms. He knew what she was saying without words. He fell onto her with a loud creak of the bedsprings. He was sure that if her aunt and uncle were awake, they would hear it, but he didn't care. He had gained the legal and moral right to do with her as he chose.

— 5 —

Early the next morning, Eliza awoke with a smile on her face. No longer did the memories of horror and pain envelope her dreams. She had new memories of passion and gentle caresses to replace the old, harsh ones. Her husband had become her lover, in word and in deed. She stretched out her arm and knew that he was gone, but she rolled to his place and drew deeply into her lungs the aroma of his maleness. It was pleasing to her. She lay satisfied and fulfilled, but soon she heard the cheerful sounds of her sisters laughing and rose to meet the new day.

It was to be a day of new sights and sounds, for Micah had hitched the wagon to a couple of horses and proclaimed he would drive Eliza and the girls into town.

"First, a treat for everyone." Micah smiled at his new wife and charges as he stopped first in front of the general store.

"What treats?" Clothilda asked shyly. She'd been quiet on the way into town.

"A sweet for my sweet ladies and maybe something extra to show off how pretty they are." He purchased them all stick candy and some ribbons for their hair, and the younger girls squealed with delight. He bought Eliza some lengths of gingham cloth, for it wouldn't be long until her other clothes would be too small for her increasing figure. He teased her about her long hair, but she knew that if she cut it tonight, he wouldn't object. She felt a new freedom in his presence that she'd never felt with her father.

When they finished their shopping, he took them to his office and showed them the empty jail cells.

"It's my job to arrest and detain mean, cruel men, and this is where they stay until the judge makes a decision about where they should go."

"Do you lock them in?" Margaret asked the question in all seriousness, seeming to remember the men from the night of the raid.

Micah assured her he did and stressed the importance of his position, but he didn't want them to grow up afraid of the Law. He showed Eliza one of the large law tomes which he'd read from cover to cover. She was impressed with his knowledge as she ran her fingers over the titles of the chapters. She was thrilled that he had taken the effort to include her sisters in his tour, for she instinctively knew he would be a good father, understanding, yet disciplined.

They drove back to the farm, with Micah pointing out interesting things to see along the way.

"See, the hill over there is where the sun first breaks through each morning. If you look just past it, you can see a tree that flowers each spring. Maybe we can have a picnic there come fall."

"In spring, too?" Clothilda asked, as she clapped and cheered.

"I'm sure spring will be a good time for a picnic, too." Eliza smiled, and she held Micah's arm with her fingers wrapped in his.

They spent the rest of the day in a leisurely manner and watched the sunset together, but the next morning he returned to town and his work. Eliza knew that it was right and just that he at least finish out his term in office. It soon became the pattern of their lives. He remained in town at his boarding house during the week but worked with Hamilton and Deming on the farm on the weekend and during those times when an additional man was needed.

The rumors of Confederate troops clashing with Federal troops didn't materialize near their area; but about sixty miles south, there was a fierce battle with many dead and wounded. Micah kept in close contact with his superiors and prayed that no harm would come to his family, as he adjusted his life to theirs. Clyde and Augusta talked of returning to their home in Kansas City but were fearful of traveling while the hostilities were so close by. The size of Eliza's belly increased, and she wore her new clothing with pride since Micah had chosen soft pale colors that brought out the gold tints in her hair. She bloomed with health. She occasionally took flowers to her father's grave and knelt in prayer, for she didn't want to forget his sacrifice for his family. Slowly, with the passing of time, the memories of that night faded from her dreams.

In the fall, the people of Crofton felt safe enough to

hold a harvest festival. All kinds of vegetables and grains were brought to be judged and weighed and bragged about. There were apples and candy for the younger girls, and Micah bought a new hat for Eliza. He never forgot that she wasn't much older than the smaller girls. He bought a jar of homemade preserves for Augusta and a cigar for Clyde. It was a precious gift because of the Union blockade, but he was told it was a local product, so it hadn't been smuggled through enemy lines. Whether he or Clyde believed it didn't matter. The gift of respect for the older man from the younger was the important blessing.

By the last of October, winter had set in for good. The wind blew cold across the prairies and fields. The harvest was good, and Clyde invested some of the money and taught Micah and Eliza how to put aside a portion of the excess funds for hard times or drought. Paris Hamilton remained at the Jennings' farm, but the other hired hand left after the harvest, for there wasn't enough work for both during the winter months. The silence on the war was a living thing; anticipation of the horror to come was felt by all the citizens of the area. But, apparently the raiders had moved farther north and west into Kansas and Nebraska Territory. Rumors of Union Army troops were heard, but none were seen. Stragglers came through one or two at a time, and an occasional horse or pig was stolen, but the people figured it was taken for food, not mischief. They began to relax as the snow drifts deepened and the ponds and creeks were frozen solid. All day and night, the aroma of burning wood permeated the air from the fires kept lighted to protect the animals and plants.

Three days before Christmas when the girls were helping Augusta churn butter, Eliza felt the first harsh pains of childbirth. Clyde volunteered to ride old Betsy the horse to town to fetch Micah, but she kept him quiet, saying it was too early yet. During the night, she gave out a loud scream, for the babe would wait no longer. Two hours later, she gave birth to her first child, a boy, and as soon as she saw him, she recalled the name of his natural father. The men had called him Ox, and the child was the image of the man. She pretended ignorance and determined to keep the secret in her heart for the rest of her days.

Micah rode to the farm as usual late on Friday afternoon, and was charmed by the greeting he received, for the child was not only born, but Eliza was already back doing her wifely chores.

"My wife, you're a new mother. You mustn't be up and about."

"Are you going to take care of the house? I feel fine," she teased as she laughed.

He scolded her for leaving her bed too early, but she didn't seem bothered, instead diverting him by asking, "We need a name for the boy. What do you think?"

"After my father, Stephen Arthur Robertson," Micah suggested.

Eliza had her doubts, for he wasn't of Micah's body, and they discussed it long into the night. Micah assured her the boy would be raised as his son, so he needed a proper name for the future. Stephen Robertson had been an honorable man, so the boy would be challenged to uphold the name of his grandfather. Micah rode back to town on Sunday night and by Monday morning, the philosophers and doomsayers were predicting disaster, for the counters of months had been right; there was no doubt but that the child was conceived that fateful night. Those pessimists were few in number, however. Most of the citizens of Claymore County praised Micah for his tolerance and compassion for the young girl who had given birth at the age of fourteen years.

Clyde Jennings filed official papers with Judge Matthews to become legal guardian of the two minor girls, over the objections of Eliza.

"Uncle, no," Eliza cried when the documents came to light.

"It's best, my dear. You have a child and a new husband." Clyde wouldn't be swayed.

Micah supported his wife in court briefs, but the judge determined that Eliza was too young to serve as guardian, and they would have more advantages with their uncle and aunt in the city. It caused a rift between the family members, and the arguments grew among them, although nothing overly serious, and they continued to function as a family. The repairs on the town house were finished by March, and Clyde began to arrange for furnishings to be sent from the city. With several items from the farm house, and a water closet built near the kitchen, there was talk of moving into the place by late spring.

Micah held his head high and didn't flinch when the child's ancestry was mentioned about the town. But, when names were posted for the election of county sheriff, his didn't appear among the chosen few. It was as well, he decided, as he had begun to suffer headaches and dizziness due to his eyes; so instead, he rented an empty building between the bakery and the doctor's surgery and opened a weapons repair shop.

"See, Eliza? It will be a fine retirement."

"It will, indeed." She walked through the building, but it was empty. "It's a small shop. Will it have work space and glass display counters as I've seen in other businesses?"

"Already ordered to be brought by wagon from Kansas City to display my wares. Shelves will be built along one wall, and in the lean to in back, a cot, a small pot-belly stove and kitchen countertop and shelves, where I can rest when I work long into the night."

"And I suppose you will work long into the night." She smiled, for she knew it was true.

"Only sometimes," he replied.

He started small, but his business grew as the men discovered his talent for repairing old revolvers and ancient rifles. The rumors of his expertise were passed along with the stage coach, and as spring progressed, his business expanded until he was able to support his family without the aid of Clyde Jennings. He continued to accept the money, however, as a means of insurance against hard times.

The headaches and dizziness grew worse, and one day in early April, Micah and Eliza took the coach to Kansas City where he saw an eye specialist.

"With surgery, I can help you, but it will be temporary with no guarantee of success," the specialist said.

Micah refused the surgery, and they returned to the farm, but kept their secret closely held in their hearts.

The baby, Stephen, grew in size and teeth. The girls were constantly admiring his good looks. There was a loud hurrah heard in town as the town crier announced the news that the war was over. The newspapers picked up the rumors, and soon the whole country knew the names, Appomattox Court House and Richmond, Virginia, from where it was said that Jefferson Davis went into hiding because a bounty was placed on the head of the former president of the Confederacy. The biggest news of all was the tale of President Lincoln's assassination in Ford's theater, and the name John Wilkes Booth went down as the most villainous creature since Judas in the Bible. The newspapers were alive daily with the trials and the hanging of the co-conspirators.

With the war over, Clyde and Augusta decided the time was right to return to their home in Kansas City.

"My dear, Eliza, you have a family now, and you've proven yourself capable of taking care of a household. It's time we left you to it." Augusta kissed her niece on the cheek on the day of their departure.

"We'll be taking the girls with us. You have your husband to consider," Clyde said, in support of his wife.

It was a sad day when they left, for the family had grown to love and admire the couple, despite their differences over the guardianship of Eliza's younger sisters. But, as Augusta insisted, she must get back to her own little grandchildren.

From his home in the city, Clyde completed the sale of the farm. The remaining furnishings that could be used were delivered to the new house. Micah and Eliza and the baby moved into the house the next week, and the loss of her family home weighed heavily on Eliza's heart.

As the summer strengthened and the weather grew warmer, the town relaxed its vigilance against raiders. The new sheriff, James McBeth, was sought out to calm all the petty quarrels and often rode to the shop to visit Micah Robertson. Yes, this same James McBeth, who had once owned the saloon and comforted the girls on the day their father was killed, had won the race for sheriff. The two men often laughed at the irony of former sheriff Micah Robertson's duty to enforce the liquor laws against the saloon, and now the saloon keeper was the sheriff and had to enforce his own laws.

When Stephen Robertson was almost a year old, his mother whispered to his father that she was with child again. It thrilled the gun repairman's heart. He loved Stephen, but his own child at the age of twenty-nine was a blessing unexpected and unprepared for. The child was another boy and was soon named John Hamilton Robertson, after the old hired man who passed away one month before his birth. Paris had suffered greatly from a growth in his stomach but hadn't told anyone about it. One day he collapsed in the barn and died the next day.

Living in the large house in Kansas City with their aunt and uncle, Margaret and Clothilda were quite the young ladies now, and almost old enough to be courted. Young men frequently seemed to be swarming around the home. Margaret, especially, had grown to be a beautiful young thing with soft brown curls and green eyes. At the age of thirteen, the same age that Eliza had been when married, it was agreed that she would enjoy a better future were she to have a finishing school education, so she was sent East to a boarding school for young ladies of her age. She was married at eighteen to a doctor in Boston. His family was very understanding when they were told that she came from Missouri and her father was killed by raiders during the dreadful war. Many men of Boston had also been lost in the conflict.

The same year that Margaret was married, Eliza gave birth to her third child, a girl named Catherine Ann Robertson. Stephen started school that fall, and his brother, affectionately called Johnie, was a lively toddler who treated his father's gun repair shop as his personal playground. When Eliza remonstrated with her husband over the dangers of playing around guns and bullets, he laughed and teased her about her hair. It was while she was with child that Eliza finally got the courage to have her hair cut very short, just above her ears. It made her small, round face quite attractive, and the men of the town would turn to take a second look at the matron who walked with two boys beside her and carrying a babe in her arms. She was both frightened and excited to visit her aunt Augusta and uncle Clyde, because of the criticism she expected about her hair from her straitlaced aunt.

It was with a great deal of surprise that the Robertsons walked into the parlor on Bright Angel Street in Kansas City and found Augusta Jennings with short, fluffy brown hair, curled and dyed with ground-up and boiled walnut shells. The last time they had seen her, the hair on top of her head was gray and long, fastened at the back by tortoise shell combs. The two women fell into each other's arms and laughed until their sides were full of pain, while the men shook their heads at the foolishness of women.

Micah and Eliza and the children stayed with Clyde and Augusta for three weeks. On one clear, brisk morning, Clothilda announced that she wanted to travel to Boston to see Margaret. It was only fair, she declared with her stubborn nose in the air, that she be given the same chance that Margaret had for a good match. Clyde, as her legal guardian, agreed that she could stay, as long as she finished her education. It was only after she had gone to Boston to visit with Margaret and her husband that Micah and Eliza heard that Clothilda had found a lover named Philip and was now with child. It turned out that Philip was already married, so there could be no chance of the father claiming the child.

Once again, Clyde took charge of the situation and found a husband acceptable for Clothilda. His name was William Parmenter, but the marriage didn't even last until the birth of the child. One day William announced that he wanted out of the agreement because he couldn't accept another man's child as his own. A divorce was quietly obtained with William awarded a large settlement for his silence on the matter, and Clothilda returned to Kansas City to give birth to her child.

The child, a girl, was born shortly after Johnie's sixth birthday and named Amarilla Eunice Parmenter and quickly given the nickname Rilla. As soon as Clothilda was healthy enough to travel, she left the child with her sister, Eliza. She attended the university and received her degree in nursing. She never remarried and followed her nursing career first to New York City and thence to Africa, where she distinguished herself with helping the poor.

When Rilla was three years old, Aunt Augusta Jennings, the matriarch of the family, died quietly in her sleep. Less than one year later, Clyde married a woman half his age and lived with her until his death at the age of two and eighty years. He was buried beside his first wife in the huge Kansas City cemetery. All his children and most of his grandchildren were beside him when he met his maker. Micah, Eliza and their children attended the funeral service. His estate was equally divided among his children with a healthy legacy for his second wife. The agreement between he and Micah remained intact as agreed, and the funds continued to be added to the Robertson account every year.

— Epilogue —

There followed a long period of peace and contentment in the Robertson household as the children grew to maturity, and Micah and Eliza grew to love and cherish their time together as a couple. Micah continued to tinker in his gun shop, but his living didn't depend on his profits from his professional endeavors, which he ran with efficiency and integrity. The profits went into the education of his children.

Eliza took her place as a member of the Ladies Aide Society of the local Methodist church and gave birth to seven more children. She enjoyed decorating the church with flowers from the garden. She learned to play the piano in her twentieth year, and the children were often seen standing around her as she pounded out the gay, modern songs or the old hymns of her youth. Christmas was a special time, with the house ringing with the sounds of laughter, the smell of spices and the evergreens with which they decorated the mantle and stairway with garlands of greenery and large red satin bows.

Micah became a member of the Town Council and served for two years, until his term expired, and served for four years as a member of the Crofton school board. In the sixth year of his career as gunsmith, he hired an assistant named Guadalupe Hays, as his eyesight grew increasingly worse. Hays was an army veteran, who with his wife Hortense, moved into a new house built on a street adjoining the Robertson home, which no longer sat alone on the prairie grass outside the town, for the town had grown beyond it for several miles. The buildings that had been damaged or destroyed by the raiders had long since been repaired or replaced, and most of the inhabitants moved away, to be replaced with settlers from the East and South, eager to escape the hardships of the past.

Catherine married a doctor and lived in Chicago. Rilla, at the age of twenty-five years, married a dentist. Micah laughed and told Eliza that the marriages took care of their health issues, for with one son-in-law a doctor and a nephew a dentist, they were set for a long future together. Johnie moved west to California and worked as a clock-maker. Surprisingly, only Stephen Robertson was interested in farming the land. He attended the university and studied animal husbandry and horticulture. At the age of thirty, he married a young woman named Glenda, and the couple built a large house on a section of land down the road about ten miles from his parents.

Crofton, which by now had grown into a sizable city,

had its own police force, run by the efficient Guy Eades from New York City. The current county sheriff worked at the huge, domed courthouse which was known to leak when a heavy rain crossed the sky. The four-story brick jail building was located about a mile away on Journey Street. For the anniversary of the construction of the courthouse, the county commissioners decided a renovation was long overdue. The exterior was refaced with pink granite, both Doric and Ionian columns were added at all the entrances, and a copper roof was overlaid over the old. It was expected to age to a soft green within a decade. For months, the repairs blocked off all entrances to the building except one and took a year to complete.

Somewhere in the drafty, high-ceilinged rooms of the large county courthouse, there was found a framed portrait of Sheriff Micah Robertson, who was the only Law officer in the isolated area for the ten years which included the Civil War. It was discovered one day by an enterprising young woman who could trace her own ancestors to that turbulent time in the nation's history. All the pictures of the previous sheriffs, including Micah's, were dusted off, new frames or glass provided, and they were hung along a wall on the second floor of the building, the third of its kind to house the county records. It showed a lean, tall man with a black mustache and gray eyes, wearing a dark suit, high stiff collar, and dark tie. He wasn't smiling.

If the young woman had bothered to ask questions about the men whose pictures she hung with such care on the walls, she would have found the same former sheriff's wife just down the road, still living in the quaint old house that used to stand alone on the prairie and attending to her spring roses. Eliza Jennings Robertson lived to the ripe old age of ninety-nine years, spry until the end, full of grace and ethereal, timeless beauty.

www.ingramcontent.com/pod-product-compliance
Lightning Source LLC
Chambersburg PA
CBHW070615130626
46556CB00001B/378